Essence of Deceit by M

ESSENCE OF DE

Outside the Old Bailey, Roland Van Mer read out a statement clearing top government official, Sir Hugh Bane-Everidge, of all charges. 'One, alleged disappearance of three young women in their twenties. Two, death of a partygoer who allegedly fell from a balcony in one of the bedrooms. Three, possession of Class A drugs with intent to supply.'

Roland continued, 'It was a great shame for all concerned. My client, Sir Hugh, is totally innocent and an upstanding member of society. Just to clarify those three points, the young ladies who disappeared had already left the Bane-Everidge Estate. The death of the young man falling from a bedroom balcony was a very unfortunate and tragic accident, and possession of Class A drugs with intent to supply is the most ludicrous thing I've ever heard. However, our sympathies go out to the young man's family and the families of the three young ladies. There is no link to Sir Hugh whatsoever. Therefore, I hope we can all move on with our lives. Thank you.'

Essence of Deceit by Mark Hall

A surge of reporters moved forwards and there was a din of questions being fired towards Sir Hugh and his lawyer. Arms, microphones and cameras in the melee.

A woman in her mid forties managed to stand on a low brick wall above the scrum. 'You bastaaaarrrddd!' she screamed, her face twisted with anger. 'Bane-Everidge, you lying bastard. I swear you'll pay for this!' She was pulled away by a burly male companion.

Another man screamed abuse but was wrestled away by a police officer. Sir Hugh and Roland scrambled and climbed into a waiting limo and were whisked away.

*

The CID team were making their way to the Old Bailey's car park. 'See you all back at the nick.' Detective Inspector Peter Thompson broke the gloomy silence.

Two cars took the team back to the police station and CID headquarters. The station was at the front of the building, with CID headquarters at the back. Peter drove one of the cars. He'd been around the block and seen it all … well, almost. He was married to Kay, who'd been in the force for eight years. She'd retired early, under a cloud of controversy and rumour. The other two in the car

Essence of Deceit by Mark Hall

were DC Spyros Papadakis, who was married and a gym fanatic and kickboxer, and DC Heather Barnes, who was married with two grown-up children. She was very clever, with a distinction from law school and more degrees than a thermometer. She was the brains of the team.

DS Dave Laing drove the other car. He was second in command and in his mid forties. He'd worked his way up through the ranks of the police force. He was a rugby enthusiast and married with two grown-up children. DC Claire Taylor and DC Bill Ferguson were the passengers. Claire was married to the force with no husband and an on-and-off boyfriend. She was a workaholic, always going the extra mile. She was about forty years old and loved cats. Bill, known affectionately as Fergus, was a Glaswegian hard cop. He was a highly respected football nut and loved Celtic. He didn't mind a wee dram.

At CID headquarters, the team got seated. Peter stared at the incident board with his hands on his hips. 'Well … the disappearance of three girls, a death, drugs. We know it's the tip of the iceberg. Rumours, whisperings … it goes on and on. The lies, the goddamn lies! It was incredible how they rolled off the tongue of that stinky crooked lawyer and that rotten piece of flesh, Sir Hugh!' Exasperated, he kicked a chair and sent it tumbling over. He looked like he was about to explode.

Spyros, in his wisdom, thought it was time to crack a joke to ease the tension. 'You aren't gonna send him a Christmas card, then?' Peter glared and raised his palm towards Spyros to indicate not now, not now.

'Unbelievable, sir. I thought we'd got Sir Hugh nailed,' said Heather.

Glaswegian Fergus was also incensed. 'The whole Bane-Everidge Estate is rotten to the core. I'd bomb the whole lot.'

Spyros then asked, 'Sir, the case is closed and the jury and court decided Sir Hugh wasn't guilty, although we all believe he is, so is that it?'

Peter pondered for a moment. 'Well, yes, he can't be done for the crimes he's been cleared of unless …' There was a silence that lasted a few seconds as the team pondered what to do next.

Usually anyone coming into the CID office knocked before they entered, but the door was flung open as Sergeant Niall Hoskins burst into the room, dropping a bombshell of news. 'Sir Hugh's lawyer, Roland Van Mendes, has been shot dead!'

'What the hell?' Dave exclaimed as he stood up from his chair. 'When? Where?' The team broke into spontaneous questions, discussions and speculations.

'Hold on, let's hear Sergeant Hoskins.'

'It only just happened. We got a call from Sir Hugh's chauffeur on his mobile. Apparently, it's a long drive on the estate up to the house. The shot went through the back window straight into the back of Van Mendes' head.' Sergeant Hoskins paused to regain his composure.

'How awful it must have been. Oh my God, oh my God! The mess ... oh, it doesn't bear thinking about,' Heather added.

Claire also joined in and asked, 'What about the others in the car?'

Sergeant Hoskins replied that it was just the chauffeur and Sir Hugh. 'They're obviously shocked and shaken, but they're okay.' He turned to leave the office and signalled to two uniformed officers by the door that it was time to go. He turned to the rest of the CID team and, in particular, Peter. 'We'll keep you posted, sir. Well, I'm sure you'll be down there very shortly.' With that, the uniform boys and the Sergeant were gone.

The office descended into a right din. 'Okay,' announced Peter, 'Dave, Spyros and Claire, you make your way down to the estate and keep me updated. Forensics will be on their way.'

*

Dave drove the car. They eventually turned into the long drive of the Bane-Everidge Estate. The occupants of the car could see the limousine ahead with all its doors open and see Sergeant Hoskins and another officer peering into the car. The CID car parked up and the trio got out. Minimal greetings were exchanged.

Sergeant Hoskins took the lead. 'Well … as you can see, the back window is gone and the victim has a bullet in the back of his head.' He winced and pulled away. Spyros moved closer to the limousine. He looked in, pulled away and was promptly sick. The victim's body was slumped against the back of the front passenger seat.

'Where are Sir Hugh and the chauffeur? Are they in the house?' asked Dave.

Essence of Deceit by Mark Hall

'Yeah, in the house. Two uniform boys are with them,' replied Sergeant Hoskins. Forensics turned up in a people carrier and there was a mad scramble to climb into light blue suits, boots and gloves. Heather started taking pictures and Spyros took notes. They looked inside and outside the limousine.

The head of forensics, Christine Canning, made her way over to the crime scene. She was greeted by Sergeant Hoskins and Dave and briefed by both officers. Christine peered in and carefully looked around the victim's head. After a few minutes, she picked out remnants of a bullet, unzipped a pocket in her overalls, pulled out a plastic bag and put the bullet in. She kept rummaging around the victim's body. Dave and Sergeant Hoskins watched in silence.

'One bullet. One shot.' It was part question, part statement.

'Apparently, according to the phone call from the chauffeur, he only heard one shot,' Dave responded. Sergeant Hoskins, Dave and Christine spent a moment contemplating the situation.

Sergeant Hoskins looked around. 'One shot. The shooter was either very lucky or a good marksman. I tend to think marksman. I reckon he came out the woods near the end of the drive. That's a good one hundred yards away. Wow! And disappeared into the woods ... gone. I'll get some of my officers and we'll scan down the end of the drive.'

'Good, okay, Sergeant Hoskins,' said Dave. 'I'll go and see Sir Hugh and the chauffeur. Spyros, you stay here with forensics. Heather, come with me, please.'

Dave and Heather walked up the steps of the grand building. The door was slightly open. They walked in and turned right along the hallway. They could hear voices and the pair of them walked into a large study. Two uniformed police officers stood up from a small two-seater settee. Sir Hugh stood with his back towards the window. The chauffeur sat in a large comfy chair looking relaxed, which was noted by Heather. She raised her eyebrows.

'It was meant for me, it was meant for me!' blurted out Sir Hugh.

'Just a moment, sir,' Dave put in. Dave and Heather exchanged brief words with the two police officers. Sir Hugh and the chauffeur were cleaned up, but they were still in the clothes which they'd worn in the limousine.

'It was meant for me, officer,' Sir Hugh repeated, now looking even more stressed.

'Whatever would give you that idea, Sir Hugh?' asked Dave.

Sir Hugh waved his arms about in irritation. 'I don't care for your sarcasm.' The change from almost hysteria to matter-of-fact calmness, even coldness, was again observed by Heather.

'Sir Hugh, tell me exactly what happened from when you left court.'

'Well, we drove through London. It takes forty-five to sixty minutes to get back to the estate.' The chauffeur sat quietly nodding in agreement.

Dave looked at the chauffeur. 'You're new here, aren't you? I've never seen you before. And your name is?'

'Diego Garcia,' replied the chauffeur.

'How long have you been working for Sir Hugh?'

'About a month,' Diego replied.

'Where are you from originally?'

'Columbia.'

'I assume you have all the relevant papers?' asked Dave.

'Of course! They are all correct and above board,' said Diego. Heather frantically made notes.

Essence of Deceit by Mark Hall

'So, Mr Garcia, did you see anything suspicious or unusual driving back? Or did you, Sir Hugh?'

Both replied almost simultaneously, 'No, nothing at all.'

Dave was still puzzled about the chauffeur. 'What happened to the other chauffeur? Hinchcliffe, wasn't it?'

'That's it, Gary Hinchcliffe. He retired down to Devon or Cornwall. Somewhere down there,' replied Sir Hugh.

Dave decided to get back to matters in hand, but made a mental note about the chauffeur. 'So, Sir Hugh, a few moments ago, you claimed that the bullet was meant for you. Could you explain a little bit more about this?'

Sir Hugh's face was a picture, a mixture of bewilderment and anger. 'My lawyer has just been murdered. I was totally shocked. It could have been me.'

Dave moved closer to Sir Hugh. 'Do go on, Sir Hugh.'

'Well, I'm probably more of a target than Roland.'

'Oh really? Have you got enemies, Sir Hugh? Have you upset people? Has someone got a vendetta? Does someone want revenge?'

Essence of Deceit by Mark Hall

It was obvious that Sir Hugh didn't like the questioning. He spoke, very curt and clipped. 'I don't know what you're implying here. I was cleared, do you understand? I was cleared of all wrongdoing. Of course, there's people who dislike me. It goes with the territory.'

'So, you've no idea who'd want to kill you then?' added Dave.

'No, I don't! You're the detective, aren't you?'

The mood was tense. Heather decided to change direction. 'Tell me, Sir Hugh, why did Gary Hinchcliffe leave?'

'I've already told you,' replied Sir Hugh. 'He went to retire in Cornwall or somewhere. He was a Neanderthal, anyway.'

'What does that mean, Sir Hugh?'

'He was working class.'

'Lower class than you, do you mean?'

'For God's sake,' replied Sir Hugh. 'All he did was drive my car. Are you going to make something out of that now?'

'Why did you hire Mr Garcia?'

Essence of Deceit by Mark Hall

'Why not?' replied Sir Hugh. 'We had a vacancy and Mr Garcia replied. It was as simple as that. Is that okay with you, officers?'

'Well, we'll look into it,' said Dave.

'I bet you will,' was Sir Hugh's sneering reply.

Dave's mobile rang. He moved slightly away to be discreet. 'Yes, yes, okay, fine. Yes, will do. We're on our way now.' He turned towards Heather. 'DI Thompson wants us back at HQ, so we'll grab Spyros and go.' He turned towards Sir Hugh and the chauffeur. 'Don't go anywhere, gentlemen. We'll be back very soon.' With that, Dave and Heather left the room.

Dave and Heather jogged down the steps and beckoned Spyros over. 'Back to base, Spyros,' shouted Dave.

Spyros and Heather made their way to the car. Dave approached Christine. 'Get the report back to me or DI Thompson when you can, Christine.'

'Ok, will do. Catch you later,' she said.

Dave drove the car slowly down the driveway. There were uniformed officers on the edge of the woods and they could see a couple more officers further in. He pulled the car over and Sergeant Hoskins walked towards the car.

Heather was sitting in the back and lowered the window. 'Any luck, Sergeant?' They all leaned forwards to hear what the Sergeant had to say.

'Nothing, absolutely nothing. We'll carry on for a bit longer.'

'Okay, Sergeant. We'll see you later,' replied Dave. The windows of the car were all wound up simultaneously and the team sped off to the station.

*

As the three detectives walked in the office, there was a hum of busyness. Heads turned towards the trio and minimal greetings were offered.

Peter came out of his small glass office. 'What are the details, Dave?' He moved to half sit on the edge of Fergus' desk. All of the team faced the three detectives.

'Roland Van Mendes was shot dead in the car by a bullet through the back window through the back of the head. At the moment, we believe the shooter to be a red-hot marksman. He came out of the woods, fired a single shot and disappeared back into the woods. There are uniformed officers scouring the area and forensics are there, as you know,' said Dave.

Peter then asked, 'What about Sir Hugh and the chauffeur?'

'They are both unharmed, but Sir Hugh believes the bullet was meant for him.'

Heather interjected, 'Sir, the chauffeur ... it's all a bit odd. He's quite new and is a Columbian called Diego Garcia. The other chauffeur, Gary Hinchcliffe, was with Sir Hugh for ten years and all of a sudden retired to Cornwall. And another thing, Diego Garcia just sat in the study after the shooting, hardly ruffled at all.' Spyros and Dave nodded in agreement.

Claire appeared in the doorway of Peter's office. 'Sir, an email has just come in.'

Peter went into his office, straight to the computer. Clare joined him and they both studied the email silently.

Detective Inspector Peter Thompson. How very unfortunate that you lost the case when more compelling evidence was staring you in the face. If you had looked hard enough instead of being blind, the guilty would be locked up doing time. Justice will be served. It won't be long. Very soon the guilty will be gone.

Peter and Claire stood in silence for a second, staring at the screen, then Peter strode into the main office and addressed the team in a loud voice. 'Okay, everyone, can I have your attention. Heads up, please. I've just received an email. It sounds like a vigilante nutjob who thinks he's Wordsworth.'

'What? Words what?' asked Spyros.

Glaswegian Fergus put his point across. 'Oh my gawd! Don't you know who Wordsworth is? Have you had too many kicks to the head with that kickboxing thing you do? He's a famous English poet.' He showed his disdain.

Peter wasn't impressed and carried on. 'So, we have—' There was a knock at the door. He didn't look happy. Christine slid in through the doorway, trying not to draw attention to herself. Peter nodded a greeting and started again. 'Now, we have a dead lawyer and a self-styled vigilante who's good with a rifle.'

Christine raised her hand. 'We know a bit more about the gunman.' Attention was now on the head of forensics. 'The bullet retrieved from the victim was almost certainly from a G3 rifle, a marksman's rifle. It's highly probable that our vigilante is a professional.'

Dave stood up. 'So Van Mendes was the intended victim, not Sir Hugh then?'

'Very likely, not definitely,' replied Christine. 'Maybe the gunman or gunwoman shot Van Mendes by mistake.'

'Why do you say gunwoman?' asked Peter.

Dave shrugged his shoulders. 'Pure speculation, I suppose…'

Spyros leaned forward to Fergus and whispered, 'DI Thompson's missus was a bit of a hot shot with a firearm.' A couple of team members stifled embarrassed laughter. It was a bad joke.

Peter heard what he'd said and glared at Spyros. It had touched a raw nerve. 'That's a very cheap shot, Spyros,' he hissed.

Immediately, Spyros realised he'd made a stupid mistake. 'Sir, I'm so sorry, very sorry.'

There was a long pause and it was quite uncomfortable in the office, then Peter said softly, 'Okay.' He looked at Spyros as though to say something then decided not to and moved back into professional mode. 'So, as Christine has pointed out, this killing bears the hallmarks of a professional, an assassin. This is what we're now dealing with. Ponder that for a moment as we grab a quick coffee.' Noise and movement filled the office.

Peter went to the water cooler and Fergus came over. 'Sir, don't take any notice of Spyros. He's a good fella though he's a bit stupid at times. I think doing that kung fu kickboxing stuff he does, he's probably had too many bashes to the head like I said earlier.' Fergus patted his boss on the shoulder.

'Yeah, no worries. I'm okay,' said Peter but Fergus could see that he was a bit sore with it.

Light conversation filled the office. Peter looked at his watch and gave the team a minute or two longer. 'Okay, can I have your attention, please. Okay, guys, it's ten o'clock. It's getting a bit late. Let's call it a day and we'll resume tomorrow at eight am sharp. Have a good night.'

The team made their way out the office, saying 'Night, boss' and 'Night, sir' as they made their way out.

*

The drive home for Peter was about thirty to forty minutes. More often than not, he would listen to jazz, normally up loud but not tonight though. He was deep in thought, not about the case, but about the comment made by Spyros about his wife. Why did he say that? Stupid berk!

He started analysing what Spyros had said, trying to make sense of it all. Kay was a wonderful wife. Fiery, yes, but she'd been excellent in the force. Yes, she'd been excellent at firearms. She'd retired early because an undercover cop had been shot dead from seventy yards from a rooftop. She'd aggressively denied shooting him. And there were those whisperings about her and Spyros. 'I don't know,' he said to himself. 'Jeeeezzz!' He let out a loud sigh.

BEEEEEPPP!

Peter was shaken back to reality by a near collision with a motorcyclist. He'd failed to indicate that he was turning right. The biker was fuming and screamed abuse at him. Christ! Better get with it, he thought. He arrived home and parked on the driveway. He locked the car, opened the front door with his key and walked in.

Kay greeted him as she came out of the lounge. 'You're late, Peter.'

'Yeah, plenty to wade through at the moment,' he replied.

'What? The Bane-Everidge case?' asked Kay.

'Yeah, it could be a marksman with a vendetta or, I don't know, a hired assassin. Someone on a revenge mission.'

'A mission?' asked Kay.

'Yeah, he, or she, sent me an email basically saying that they would do the job that the police hadn't.' Kay didn't answer, but Peter knew what she thought about the police and it was mostly scathing. He moved to the fridge. 'I'm starving. What've we got?'

'Shepherd's pie. It's all ready. Just microwave it. I'm off to bed, Peter. Try not to wake me.' Kay blew him a kiss. 'Night.'

'Night, love,' he replied.

Peter eventually climbed into bed, exhausted. Soon he was in a deep sleep, but his blissful sleep was shattered by his mobile phone ringtone at three am. It was Dave.

'Sir, there's been another shooting at the Bane-Everidge Estate.'

'Okay, Dave. Give me the details.'

'One of the kitchen staff has been shot dead. He'd just been dropped off by a taxi and was walking to his sleeping quarters. Uniformed officers and an ambulance are on their way right now.'

Peter replied, 'I'm on my way.' He dressed and was ready to go in minutes. He kissed Kay on the top of her sleeping head, was out the door and gone. In his car, he turned the music on and up loud. It was Oasis.

Essence of Deceit by Mark Hall

Peter eventually arrived at the end of the long drive of the Bane-Everidge Estate. At the top of the driveway, he could see two squad cars and an ambulance. He could also see Dave, who was in conversation with a uniformed officer.

He parked his car and as he climbed out, Dave and Sergeant Glen Peters walked over to him. They exchanged a quick greeting and Sergeant Peters walked the two CIDs to the crime scene. 'The victim is just around the corner,' he said. 'It's awful.'

Within a minute or two, they were faced with a body covered in a white sheet. Sergeant Peters took up the proceedings. 'Shot in the forehead.' Peter pulled the sheet back and the three officers winced.

'We're guessing he was shot between two-thirty and three am. Apparently, a taxi dropped him off here about two-twenty-five. The victim had been clubbing in town. We've contacted the taxi company and spoken to the driver. He saw nothing,' said Sergeant Peters.

Peter asked, 'Who made the call to the police?'

'The butler found him,' replied the Sergeant. 'We've spoke to the butler at length, although, obviously, we need to question everybody.'

Dave asked, 'What do we know about the victim?'

Sergeant Peters continued, 'Apparently, he was a chef and in his mid thirties. He was a popular fella. His name was Ben Charles. He was single and from Newcastle. He'd been working for about six years for Sir Hugh and was reliable and decent.'

Peter started to direct proceedings. 'Okay, let's convene in the main study. I think we know where it is by now. I want all the staff there. If they're not awake, then wake them up. We're going to do a roll call. Also wake up Sir Hugh.'

'I'm already here.' Sir Hugh walked towards the officers dressed in a silk dressing gown. 'Dreadful business, detectives. This is terrible.' Peter and Dave nodded their heads in agreement.

Sergeant Peters and two of his uniformed officers moved off to wake up the staff. While two uniformed officers taped off the crime scene, Peter and Dave walked with Sir Hugh towards the main building. Members of staff had started filtering into the main study.

Sir Hugh sat in the main leather chair. Dave was ready to take notes. Two uniformed officers made their way in.

Peter was ready to commence. 'Is everybody here?'

'Almost,' came the reply from housekeeper Janice Brown. The room had an atmosphere of disbelief and shock. Quiet sobbing could be heard.

'Well, my colleagues and I are truly sorry about this latest tragedy,' said Peter. With that, one of the young girls started wailing and was comforted by Janice. 'I'm sorry to drag you in here, but I need to assess everybody's whereabouts. Sir Hugh, could you please do a quick roll call, thanks.'

'I have here my trusted butler, Reggie Milner, who runs the place. The general housekeepers are the fantastic Janice Brown, God bless her, the brilliant Mary Edmunds and Gina Fitzsimmons. The brilliant kitchen staff are Phil Atkins, Jed Mullins and Carl Watts.' Sir Hugh took a visible deep breath. 'And Ben was great.'

The atmosphere was awful. A bit more sobbing could be heard. Sir Hugh wiped an eye, struggled for a moment, then regained his composure and soldiered on. 'Diego Garcia, my chauffeur, and last, but not least, Archie Sangster, DIY man, builder, general

Essence of Deceit by Mark Hall

problem solver and virtuoso gardener.' Sir Hugh then groaned, 'Where the hell is he?'

Dave discreetly nudged Peter and whispered, 'Virtuoso gardener!' He rolled his eyes skywards. Peter replied with a grin.

The butler, Reggie, moved forwards. 'Don't worry, Sir Hugh. I'll deal with this. Archie, the silly old sod, is probably too drunk to wake up.'

Peter stepped in. 'Don't worry. I'll send one of our officers over.'

'He's not in the main quarters. He's done up his gardener's shed and sleeps in there,' Sir Hugh pointed out.

'Thanks, that's a great help,' replied Peter. He nodded to one of the uniformed officers, who left the study. He decided to wait until everybody was present before they carried on with their enquiries.

Shortly after, the door was opened and Archie Sangster joined the group. He shuffled in. He had a slight hunch on the left side of his back and although he wasn't in great shape, it had never been a problem in his day-to-day work. But, apparently, he liked a drink.

Essence of Deceit by Mark Hall

'So, we're finally all here now?' Peter exclaimed.

Archie asked, 'What's up? What's going on?' He wasn't fully awake or really with it. Dave was irritated. 'You've obviously not heard, have you? There's been another shooting.'

Archie looked like a ghost. 'Oh my God! Who? Where?'

Reggie joined in the conversation. 'It was Ben, the chef. He was shot. He was shot…' He struggled with his emotions. '…by the sleeping quarters.' Archie shuffled forwards to find a seat.

Peter counted the group quietly, gesticulating with his right hand. 'So, we have a group of nine?' He looked at Sir Hugh for confirmation, who nodded his head in agreement. 'Anybody hear anything? See anything?' Blank faces and shaking heads were the response. The two CIDs looked intently and slowly around the group.

Dave continued, 'So no one heard anything or saw anything?' He turned his attention to the butler. 'Mr Milner, you said you went for a cigarette and a breath of fresh air at around three am?'

'Yes, that's right,' replied Reggie.

Essence of Deceit by Mark Hall

Dave continued, 'Well, why didn't you just open a window for a fag and a breath of fresh air?'

'I wasn't sleeping that great. There's no light pollution up here so I decided to stretch my legs and have a good look at the stars as well.'

'Do carry on, Mr Milner,' interjected Peter.

'Yeah ... I walked around the corner...' Reggie rummaged through his pockets and found a handkerchief. He blew his nose loudly. 'And there was Ben. I looked at him and...' Reggie paused for a moment. 'I realised he was dead. It was terrible, I looked around. Everywhere was quiet. It seemed too quiet.'

Janice spoke up for the group. 'Well, at three o'clock in the morning I guess most people are asleep, you know. We all do fairly long days. It's quiet up here so we sleep like logs. I'm sorry we haven't been much help, officers. This is just terrible.'

'It most certainly is,' Sir Hugh added.

Peter addressed the group. 'If anybody thinks of any small detail, however trivial, please let me know.' He put a card on the table. 'My phone number is on here. You can ring me direct. Thank you for your help. Just to repeat, do not hesitate to call me if you think of anything. We will speak again very shortly. Uniformed police are on duty tonight. Thanks again.'

Peter and Dave left the building. Forensics were with the victim and the two CIDs walked over to them.

'What have you got, Christine?' enquired Peter.

'A head shot. The same bullet as the other victim, Roland Van Mendes. It's quite secluded up here so, as a calculated guess, the marksman was hiding in the woods. He came out. Boom! Gone.' The detectives and forensics nodded in agreement at the now strong possibility.

Peter sighed deeply. 'I'll contact you tomorrow, Christine.'

'Well, it is tomorrow,' mentioned Dave.

'Okay, later today then. I'll speak to Sir Hugh and they can notify the next of kin.'

Peter and Dave made their way to their cars. Sergeant Peters came over with an update. 'We've scoured everywhere. There's nothing, absolutely nothing.'

Sergeant Peters and the two CID officers stood by the cars. 'Okay, it's six am now. I'm going home for a coffee and a shower,' said Peter.

'Ditto that,' replied Dave.

'See you back at the office about eight.' Peter turned to Sergeant Peters. 'Keep me posted.'

Will do, sir,' replied the Sergeant.

*

In the office, later that morning, all six members of CID were in attendance. Peter moved towards a big board on the wall, the evidence board, the central reference point. He picked up a cloth and wiped it clean. There were felt tip pens in a box attached to the board in precise order. Everyone knew that if you wanted to upset the boss, then let him try to find a felt pen when he needed one.

Peter began, 'So, to date, two killings – Roland Van Mendes, the lawyer, and Ben Charles, the chef. At this moment in time, this bears all the hallmarks of an assassin.' The rest of CID shuffled in their seats with expressions of quite likely and nods of agreement. 'Dave, Heather, Clare and Spyros, please can you guys go back to the Bane-Everidge Estate. Have a poke around. Question the staff individually. Chat to the chauffeur. Also, inquire about the first chauffeur, Gary Hinchcliffe, who supposedly retired. Fergus and I will remain in the office here. Any questions?'

Claire asked, 'Any news on that email, sir?'

'No nothing as yet. The tech boys have tried tracing it but they've had no luck. We haven't received any more emails either.' There was a knock at the door and Peter shouted, 'Yeah?'

Christine walked in. She stood at the front by the evidence board and held up two small clear plastic bags, a spent bullet in each one. 'Identical bullets in both victims. Most certainly the same firearm and most certainly the same perpetrator. I can't really add a great deal. The targets were most likely chosen and not random.'

Peter expressed his opinion. 'That confirms it then. An assassin. Hired or self-motivated? Was it revenge?' Christine moved away from the board and Peter wrote down exactly what he'd said in bold black felt pen.

There was another knock at the door and Sergeant Peters walked in. 'I'm just knocking off night duty, sir. Sergeant Hoskins is at the Bane-Everidge Estate now with another team.'

'That's great,' replied Peter. 'It's nice to have uniform down there. It calms the nerves of the occupants. Anything to report?'

'No, nothing, sir,' came the reply from Sergeant Peters.

'That sounds familiar,' Dave said in a hushed voice.

Peter decided it was time for action. 'Right. You know what to do. Good luck.' The four CIDs dragged their chairs back and made the way out the office. Christine stood back and looked at the board.

'What are your thoughts, Christine,' asked Peter.

'Phew, I don't know ... Okay, Roland Van Mendes was eliminated. He was a very slippery individual.'

'Yeah, total scum,' added Fergus, using no-nonsense Glaswegian language. 'I could see a lot of people queuing up to get rid of him. Horrid individual. But, the young fella, the chef, Ben Charles. What did he do? Dish up some shite food?' Christine didn't quite get Fergus's sense of humour and her glance to Peter confirmed that.

Fergus didn't care at all. He'd seen the rough and tough end of the Gorbals in Glasgow. He was on a roll. 'How come Sir Hugh hasn't been bumped off already? Answer me that one. He's the one in the middle of all this. Anyway, that's my opinion.'

Peter spoke, 'We do seem to have a professional hitman doing the job. Maybe Sir Hugh's not on the list.'

'A list, guvnor?' asked Fergus. 'I sincerely hope not.'

Peter had a very uneasy feeling and it wouldn't be long before he felt worse. Fergus, Peter and Christine pondered in silence for a few seconds.

'Gentlemen, I'm off. Keep me updated.' Christine marched out of the office.

Peter watched Christine leave. Fergus spotted this and said, 'Nice, isn't she? Anyway, sir, you're a married man.' The pair of them laughed like schoolboys and made their way into Peter's private office.

Peter went to his computer. He could see there was a new email in the inbox. He opened the email.

I WILL K

'Is that it?' exclaimed Fergus. 'I will what? I will k…keep? Kill? Know?' Fergus didn't get it and shook his head.

Peter, who'd been quietly studying the email, decided to voice his opinion. 'Perhaps the person was interrupted or it's cryptic?' He kept staring at the screen.

Fergus had done enough brain searching. 'I can't see cryptics. I think it means sod all.'

Essence of Deceit by Mark Hall

Peter kept staring at the screen as though virtually hypnotised. He wanted an answer. A trickle of dread seeped into his thinking like a poisonous cloud. He pushed at the thought, his mind starting to churn. No, hell no! he thought. God, don't let this be true. He was beginning to think that his wife Kay was involved. Quite often she would leave notes in the kitchen, or sometimes on a Christmas present tag, with the initial 'K'.

Fergus caught sight of Peter. 'Sir, sir, are you okay? You don't look too good.'

'I'm okay, thanks. I guess it was sent by mistake. Nothing really on it.'

'Come on, boss,' said Fergus. 'Let's go and get coffee. That'll make you feel better.' He looked at Peter again. 'Are you sure you're all right, sir?'

'Yeah, fine, Fergus. Thanks for your concern. Now go and make the coffee.' Fergus started to fill the kettle in the small kitchen area. 'I'm just gonna to nip to the bathroom,' declared Peter.

In the toilet, he rinsed his face with cold water, leaned on the sink and stared into the mirror. His thoughts returned to the email. It was impossible that it was Kay. Impossible. He mentally reran his wife's time in the force. Kay had been dismissed about three years ago. No one had got the total truth out. An undercover cop had been shot dead. He'd been yards from apprehending a criminal. The criminal had also been shot dead. There'd been no witnesses on the warehouse rooftop and the other cops on the operation missed the incident by minutes.

The finger of suspicion had pointed straight at Kay. Nothing had been proved and Kay had been forced into early retirement. The undercover cop who'd been shot had been named Greg Mulgrove. The rumour was that Kay and Greg had hated each other with an intense passion. This was vehemently denied by Kay. The controversy and rumours had persisted for some time. They'd eventually died down but had never gone away. Kay never spoke about the incident, and she was very bitter towards the police.

Kay now worked in a florists. She seemed happy enough. It was stupid to think that Kay was involved. Just impossible all round. Peter almost felt like giving himself a rollicking. He then took some more cold water, brushed his hands through his hair, stood up straight and wiped his hands dry.

Essence of Deceit by Mark Hall

Peter marched back to the office and into the kitchen area.

'Coffee is served,' announced Fergus. 'You don't take sugar, sir, do you?'

'No,' replied Peter.

'Thought not,' said Fergus. 'You're sweet enough.'

*

Dave, Heather, Spyros and Claire were on the steps of the grand house of the Bane-Everidge Estate. Dave pressed the doorbell. Seconds later the butler, Reggie, opened the door. Dave flashed his credentials automatically and the four of them went in.

'We need to ask a few more questions,' instructed Dave. Reggie shuffled on the spot, looking uncomfortable.

'You okay?' Dave asked.

'Yes, I'm fine, It's just very … er … disturbing, these killings. So scary. Roland and then Ben. And … er … yeah, it's terrible.'

The five of them were standing in the hall. Heather responded instantly to what Reggie had just said. Her suspicions had rocketed. 'What did you just say? Repeat that.

Essence of Deceit by Mark Hall

You said Roland and Ben then hesitated. Are you hiding something, Mr Miller?'

'No, no, not at all. And it's Mr Milner, Reggie Milner.'

'Wait here, Mr Milner,' instructed Dave. 'I'll inform Sir Hugh that we're here.'

He walked through to the lounge and met Sir Hugh. The greetings were quite friendly. 'Hello, Sir Hugh.'

'Hello, Detective Laing.'

'We have a few more questions to ask. We'll probably speak to everybody individually in due course. At the moment, I wish to speak to your chauffeur, Diego Garcia, and your butler, Reggie Milner.' Sir Hugh suggested the dining room. 'Well, if you don't mind, Sir Hugh, we'd like two officers in the study and two in the dining room.'

'Is that really necessary?' protested Sir Hugh.

'Sir Hugh, please help us with our inquiries.'

'Of course, yes, of course.' Sir Hugh was slightly apologetic.

'Okay, we'll get on with it.' Dave turned on his heel and walked away. He was slightly irritated by the initial lack of cooperation from Sir Hugh and muttered to himself, 'Goddamn upper class twit.' In the hall, he got organising. 'Spyros and Claire, you start with the chauffeur, Diego Garcia, in the dining room.'

Reggie moved forwards. 'I'll get him for you.'

'Oh no, you won't, Mr Milner. Come with me and DC Barnes. We're off to the study.' Dave spoke to Spyros, 'Go and get the chauffeur.'

Sir Hugh appeared, hovering around. 'If you want tea or coffee or something, I'll instruct the staff.'

Dave showed his appreciation. 'How very nice. Coffee for me and coffee for DC Papadakis. I'm sure DC Taylor would like coffee. What about you DC Barnes?'

'No thanks. I'm fine.'

'Okay,' replied Sir Hugh. 'I'll notify one of the staff to sort it out.' He walked away.

Dave and Heather escorted Reggie to the study. Dave arranged a small dining table with two chairs side by side on one side of the table and a single chair on the other side. 'Take a seat please, Mr Milner,' he said.

'No, thank you, sir. I'd rather stand. Why am I being interrogated?'

Dave started to feel irritated with the butler. 'Mr Milner, we're going to ask you a few questions, that's all. You may be aware of two murders that happened here recently. It will make it easier all round if you cooperate.'

There was a knock at the door and in walked Janice with coffee and two glasses of water on a tray. There was also a small dish of the kind of fancy-looking biscuits that look good but taste awful.

Heather thanked Janice for the refreshments. 'There's a glass of water here, Mr Milner. Do you want one, or a biscuit?' she said.

'Nope.'

'Why's that then? Lost your appetite?'

Heather decided to take the initiative and open the questioning. She felt that Dave had started off on the wrong foot. 'Mr Milner. Can I call you Reggie?'

'I'd rather you didn't,' came the butler's terse reply.

Heather continued, 'When I spoke to you earlier, you said there were three killings?'

'Absolutely not! I never said that at all. You're making things up.'

Essence of Deceit by Mark Hall

'Well, Mr Milner. When we first entered the building and spoke to you, you said how awful the killings were and mentioned Roland and Ben. And then you hesitated, didn't you?' Heather kept pushing.

Reggie grabbed a chair and sat opposite the two detectives. He folded his arms. There was a moment's silence, then Dave leaned towards Reggie and asked in a strong slow whisper, 'Are you hiding something from us, Mr Milner?'

'No, I'm not.'

There was a knock at the door. 'Yeah,' replied Dave.

Claire poked her head round the door. 'Sorry to bother you, DS Laing, but Diego Garcia, the chauffeur, has gone out, apparently into London shopping.'

'Okay,' huffed Dave. 'Interview the housekeeper, Janice Brown.'

'Okay, will do.' Clare shut the door.

Dave continued with the butler, 'Mr Milner, any idea what happened to Gary Hinchcliffe? He was here for ten years, wasn't he?'

Reggie shuffled in his seat. Heather watched his every movement for a sign, a tell or a give-away. 'He retired to Cornwall, I believe,' replied Reggie.

Dave raised his voice. 'You believe? Don't you know for certain? You knew him for ten years. How do you know he retired to Cornwall?'

'Sir Hugh told me,' replied Reggie.

'Don't you keep in contact with Gary?' asked Heather.

'No I don't,' Reggie replied. 'He just retired and left. I suppose he wanted to start a new life.'

'Or did he just disappear?' Dave prompted.

'Look, I don't know his business. I've told you everything I know.'

Dave went into hard cop mode again. He moved his face forwards menacingly towards Reggie. 'Listen here and listen well. This whole place is like a secret goddamn society. All the previous business with three young ladies disappearing, a young lad's death, drugs, and everything else that went on. Now we have two shootings. Are you or are you not the butler? You must see all the comings and goings of everyone around here?'

Essence of Deceit by Mark Hall

Reggie stood up abruptly. 'You're harassing me. You're bullying me. I'm going to file a complaint.'

Heather stood up too and said in a soft voice, 'Come on, Mr Milner. Sit down again and take a deep breath.' Dave moved to get the glasses of water. Reggie stood behind his chair. It was tense. Heather held out a hand with a gentle gesture and beckoned Reggie to sit down again. She took the water from Dave and gave a glass to Reggie. It was a strained interview.

Slowly, Reggie sat down. Heather mouthed a quiet thank you to him and he responded with a small smile.

*

The killer waited. Patience was a virtue. Timing was everything. A breeze was blowing through the trees and the killer blended in with the surroundings. The rifle was set. The silencer was on. The killer crouched behind a tree in a small copse on the far side of the house. The living quarters were in view, about seventy yards away. A nice secluded area for a hit. The killer had previously been in a similar spot, quite near, when the chef was eradicated. The next target wouldn't be long in coming…

*

Essence of Deceit by Mark Hall

In the study, the mood had eased. 'Can I go now?' asked Reggie.

The two detectives looked at each other. 'Fine by me,' said Dave.

'Yeah, fine,' said Heather. Reggie stood up and left the room.

'What do you think?' Dave asked Heather.

'We didn't get much, did we?' said Heather. 'We're no wiser about the chauffeur, and, as you said, he must see everything that goes on here.'

'Do you know what?' said Dave. 'I think there's a film in the 1950s or even earlier about what the butler saw. He must have seen something. Maybe he doesn't know about the chauffeur, or maybe he does. I think he's hiding something. We'll question him again, no doubt.'

There was a knock at the door and in walked Clare and Spyros. Dave and Heather stood up. The four detectives decided to have a brief run through of the finished interviews.

Claire spoke first. 'We didn't get anything from Janice Brown. Obviously, she's still upset from the killings. She did say that parties and gatherings here were pretty wild.' 'Though there was no wrongdoing, apparently,' Spyros added. Dave pulled a face which virtually said that if you believed that then you'd believe anything.

They continued to discuss and chew over what they'd learned from Janice Brown and Reggie Milner.

*

Janice nipped back to her living quarters, which were situated on their own. The nearest buildings to the living quarters were the kitchen, the laundrette, and buildings that were generally used to run the house. The buildings were tucked out the way so as not to interfere with the beauty of the Bane-Everidge house.

Janice was desperate for a cigarette. She went into her living quarters to get her cigarettes then came straight out again and bumped into Reggie. They shared cigarettes and talked over recent events. Janice gave Reggie a cigarette.

'I can't stand all of this,' Janice opened the conversation. She inhaled deeply on her cigarette and Reggie lit his. 'It must be worse for you because you found Ben. How terrible! What the hell is going on?' Janice continued. Reggie listened but didn't speak, just kept puffing and flicking his cigarette. 'All this stuff before the shootings. The wild, wild parties, those three young girls disappearing, and the young guy who "fell off the balcony".' Janice made air quotes with her fingers then fumbled in her pocket for another cigarette.

'Here, have one of mine,' Reggie offered. He then carried on the discussion. 'I think they're still here … CID. That bunch of toe rags, with that bloke Lane or Laing.'

'It's Laing, DS Laing,' corrected Janice.

'Anyway,' Reggie continued, 'that Laing geezer. Gets right out of his pram. Thinks he's some hard nut. Bloody git!'

'What do you mean, Reggie?' asked Janice.

'He starts losing it, getting angry with me and saying things like, "You're the butler. You should know everybody and everything." For God's sake!' Reggie puffed out a big cloud of smoke.

'Well, you found Ben…'

'Yeah, I know, I know.' Reggie threw the fag end of his cigarette onto the floor and screwed his foot on it. 'I told the woman detective everything again. About finding Ben out the back here. I don't know anything. Just because I'm the butler, they think I did it. I know Ben liked the white powder a bit…'

Essence of Deceit by Mark Hall

'Mm, yeah,' agreed Janice. 'He was alright though. I thought he was a decent bloke.' She paused for a moment and let out a big sigh. 'I'll miss him.'

'Yeah, I will too,' agreed Reggie. 'I'll tell you who I really didn't like. That creepy slimy pervert Roland Van Mendes. I don't like Sir Hugh's friend, Clive Villiers, either. He's well dodgy.'

Janice gave a mock shiver. 'Urggghh! Everyone reckons it's an assassin doing these shootings,' she declared.

'Yeah, quite possible. Yeah, probable, I would say. Who reckons that anyway?' asked Reggie.

'Well, the girls do, Gina and Mary, and the boys in the kitchen, Phil and Jed. I'm not sure about Carl. Archie said he didn't give a toss providing he wasn't on the list and he still got paid.'

Reggie roared with laughter and Janice giggled as well. 'He's a right one. Was he drunk again?' he enquired.

'I don't know,' replied Janice. 'He does make me laugh. He's like the hunchback of the Bane-Everidge Estate shuffling about.'

'His hump ain't that big. The way you're talking, anyone would think he was Quasimodo. I don't think it's a hump, anyway. I think it's where he keeps his Jack Daniels,' replied Reggie and the pair started giggling again.

Janice drew deeply on the last bit of her cigarette. Her mobile phone started to ring. She threw the remnants of her cigarette onto the floor and turned her head away from Reggie to receive the call. 'Yes, yes, okay.' She indicated to Reggie that she had to go and she was in a rush. She jogged to the main building while still talking on the phone.

*

The killer was very still and patient. The killer knew the odds with four detectives in the vicinity. The job HAD to be done. The housekeeper and the butler were together longer than the killer had anticipated. The killer watched silently as the woman moved away and thought that it was about time. They were finally separated. The butler was in no rush to leave. He adjusted his tie and pulled out a comb from a pocket inside his jacket. The killer looked through the telescopic lens, aimed at the back of the target's head, then squeezed the trigger. The butler toppled forwards. Gone. Erased. The killer had done the job. The rifle was taken apart quickly and the telescope and silencer bagged up. The killer disappeared into the surrounding woods without any noise or disturbance.

*

Janice went into the house, heading for Sir Hugh's office. As she went past the study, the four CID officers came out. 'Janice, we need to speak to the gardener, Archie Sangster. Also, is Diego Garcia, the chauffeur, back from London yet?' asked Dave.

'I don't know about Diego. If you hold on a couple of minutes, I've just got to see Sir Hugh then I'll get Archie.'

At that moment, Sir Hugh came along the corridor. 'Ah, Janice, just a moment. How's it going, officers?'

'We've spoke to Reggie Milner and Janice. We need to speak to Archie Sangster and Diego Garcia,' Dave explained.

Sir Hugh quietly put his hands together. 'Diego will be turning up any moment. He's picking up my friend, Clive Villiers. We're having early evening drinks, followed by a lovely evening meal.'

'How nice,' interjected Spyros with a slight hint of sarcasm that went over Sir Hugh's head. But not Claire's and she gave him a look.

'Yes, it will be lovely. Janice, we'll have the usual drinks at about five-thirty and as it's a lovely evening, we'll have them on the patio outside the dining room. We'll have the meal in the dining room.'

'I'll go and arrange the patio, then I'll be off to the kitchen,' said Janice. 'Oh, I just remembered, I'm supposed to get Archie for the detectives to speak to.'

'Surely the detectives can go and find Archie?' Sir Hugh suggested.

'Fine by us,' Dave replied. 'Spyros and Claire, you can find Archie Sangster. Heather and I will wait for Diego Garcia.'

Sir Hugh then explained to the two detectives where they would find the gardener. 'I think Archie is round the back of the house, fixing one of the greenhouses. Go back to the lounge, through the patio doors and across the patio. Then down the steps and along the large privet hedge that runs alongside the swimming pool. Follow the hedge round to the left and the greenhouses are not that far from there. I'm sure you'll find him.' Spyros and Claire moved off.

Essence of Deceit by Mark Hall

The doorbell rang. 'That must be Clive now,' said Sir Hugh sounding excited. The bell rang again with an agitated sound. Sir Hugh asked, 'Where is that butler? Do I have to do everything around here?'

*

Spyros and Claire walked through the lounge doors, across the patio and down the steps. The patio was a grand affair. At the bottom of the steps, Spyros turned to look at the house. 'It's pretty glorious,' he said. 'And the patio ... Wow! I love those two little fountains, the one outside the lounge and the one outside the dining room. They really complement the patio. They're not too big ... I guess they're about four foot. They look like goddesses or angels holding up the world.'

Clare added, 'You think you're a Greek god with all those muscles you've got, don't you, Spyros?'

'Ha ha, I wish!'

They could see Janice arranging chairs and setting the table for evening drinks. Spyros remarked, 'How the other half live.'

Essence of Deceit by Mark Hall

Janice completed her task and walked back into the dining room. Dave and Heather were getting set up in there with Diego Garcia.

*

Sir Hugh and Clive chatted noisily as they stepped on to the patio. 'Clive, make yourself comfortable. Someone will bring the drinks in a moment. I'll be with you in five minutes. I'm just taking a call.' Sir Hugh went through the door into the lounge, saying, 'Now, where's that butler?'

Clive sat at the patio table, bending and folding a serviette. Mary walked onto the patio with a tray with two tumblers filled with ice and lemon. Also on the tray was a decanter of gin, two medium-sized bottles of tonic water and a bowl of nibbles. She stood by the table. Clive cast aside the serviette and Mary placed the tray down on the table. 'There you are, Mr Villiers. Shall I pour it for you?'

'No, thank you.'

Mary arranged everything in a proper and correct manner. There were no half measures here, not even with the drinks. Mary and Clive did not engage in conversation. Mr Villiers was far too aloof to engage in tittle-tattle with the staff.

Essence of Deceit by Mark Hall

The evening sun was lovely and warm. This was upper class tranquillity. Clive took a large swig of his gin and tonic, eased back in his chair, and momentarily shut his eyes. A gentle breeze blew across the patio and altered the noise of the fountain as the flow of water changed direction. After a couple of minutes, Clive sat up in his chair and had another mouthful of gin and tonic. He began to wonder how long Sir Hugh was going to be.

*

Spyros and Claire were at the swimming pool area. It was a gorgeous sight to behold with crystal clear water, luxurious sun loungers, a shower area and quaint changing facilities, all enclosed with an eight-foot garden wall. There were pretty flowers in small alcoves in the wall and a couple of hanging baskets.

'Will you get a load of this!' Spyros exclaimed.

'Nice, very nice,' Claire agreed.

'I'm gonna dive in and have a quick swim. Come on, Claire, come and join me.'

'Are you absolutely mad? Spyros, we're on duty. We're supposed to be finding the gardener, Archie Sangster, plus you've got no swimming gear,' Claire protested. 'If Dave found out about this, you'd be suspended and God knows what would happen if DI Thompson found out. You'd probably be booted out for good. Come on, stop fooling around.'

Spyros wasn't listening. 'Come on, Claire. It's been a hot day. I'll do two quick lengths. I've got boxers on. It's about half the size of an Olympic swimming pool, about twenty-five yards. It'll take no time.' Spyros was out of his clothes in seconds. SPLOSH! And in. He swam four strokes front crawl, then turned on his back kicking the water up. 'This is great!' he exclaimed, then turned onto his front and proceeded to do front crawl again.

Claire reluctantly picked his clothes up and grabbed a towel off a sun lounger. She was fuming.

*

On the patio, Sir Hugh poked his head around the door. 'I'm so sorry, Clive. I'll be two more minutes and then I'll be with you.'

'No problem, Sir Hugh. No problem at all.'

*

The killer assessed the situation. There was noise from the pool and a good view of the patio. Nice big manicured hedges for cover. But the odds were getting worse for the killer. The killer cursed under

Essence of Deceit by Mark Hall

their breath. The four detectives were still there. The two clowns mucking about in the pool … that wasn't in the equation … and the other two in the house. How much longer would it be before the butler was found? The killer eased along the hedge, conscious of the two detectives in the pool area. Let's get this job done. The killer slid into the hedge as much as possible, without impeding their vison of the next target. Clive Villiers was picking at the bowl of nibbles. The killer aimed the rifle at the target, looked through the scope with pinpoint precision to the side of the head and squeezed the trigger. Phutt! A muted sound was released. Villiers and his chair crashed sideways, knocking drinks over as he fell. Glass. Blood. Carnage. The killer looked at the house for a millisecond and said goodbye then moved swiftly backwards, keeping close to the hedge. The killer moved round the back and disappeared.

*

Spyros was walking up the steps of the pool. He flexed his bicep muscles in a pose. 'Greek god or what?'

'Yes, you're lovely,' Claire said very sarcastically. 'Now get these ruddy clothes on before we both get sacked.'

Essence of Deceit by Mark Hall

A woman's high-pitched scream punctured the air. Within seconds, a man's voice could be heard shouting for help from a totally different direction to the woman.

Spyros scrambled out of the pool. Claire threw the towel at him. 'You're a total idiot,' she shouted. 'Something's bloody well happened and we're down here. And to make matters worse, we haven't got Archie Sangster yet. We're up to our necks in it and it's all down to you, you clown.'

Spyros said nothing. He turned his back on Claire as he dropped his boxers and tried quickly to dry off and get dressed.

'Goddamn hurry up,' Clare growled.

'Okay, okay,' Spyros murmured. He was hobbling about trying to put socks on, which wasn't a great sight.

Claire was still stressed. 'I can't believe this!' she blurted. Spyros was dressed now, his boxer shorts rolled up in a towel and slung onto a sun lounger. They ran along the hedge towards the commotion on the patio. They got to the steps and ran up them.

'Oh my God, oh my God!' Spyros mumbled. The seriousness of the situation was beginning to emerge.

'Hell's bells!' Claire said.

Essence of Deceit by Mark Hall

They were greeted by the sight of somebody lying on their back and Mary and Gina attending to the prone victim on the ground.

Sir Hugh came and greeted the detectives. He was very distressed. 'Somebody shot him. Somebody shot my friend Clive. Somebody shot him.' Dazed and confused, Sir Hugh just stood there.

Claire took Sir Hugh and gently led him to a chair. Spyros approached the body. Mary and Gina had done their very best but it was hopeless. There was nothing more they could do. Clive Villiers had been shot clean through the head. Mary stood up, while Gina continued to try to clean up the awful, tragic mess.

'Okay, okay. I'm sorry but you'd best leave everything. Forensics might miss something if you clean up,' Spyros said and held out his hand for Gina.

'I can't leave him like this. I just can't. It's not right. It's… it's…' Gina struggled for words.

Mary helped Spyros to get Gina on her feet. 'We'll cover him with a sheet,' she said quietly.

'Who found him?' Spyros asked.

'I did,' came the reply from Sir Hugh. He stood up and walked towards Spyros. 'I'd been on the phone. I came out to join Clive and this had happened.'

Heather stumbled through the patio doors. 'Oh my God!' she cried as she looked at the victim. 'This is just unbelievable. This is madness.' She put her hand to her open mouth.

'It's Clive Villiers,' Spyros pointed out.

Heather broke the news. 'There's been another shooting. Reggie Milner's been shot dead as well.'

Everybody on the patio looked shell-shocked. Sir Hugh was the first to speak. 'Is this gunman trying to pick everybody off?'

Heather did her best to explain to her colleagues, Sir Hugh and the two staff members what had happened to the butler. 'DS Laing and I were questioning the chauffeur, Diego Garcia, in the dining room. We heard a commotion outside the house and then almost at the same time we heard disturbing sounds from this direction. As we left the dining room, Carl Watts virtually ran into us. He told us that he and Jed Mullins had found Reggie Milner dead. He'd been shot through the back of the head.'

Essence of Deceit by Mark Hall

'God, it's crazy!' exclaimed Gina and promptly burst into tears. Mary put her arm round her and tried to console her.

'Where was Reggie found?' asked Mary.

'By the staff living quarters,' replied Heather. 'DS Laing is there now.'

*

Dave was agitated. He tried to ring Spyros and Claire, but the phone signal was weak up by the living quarters. Jed had explained that the signal seemed to come and go and that some days were better than others. Dave then tried to phone Heather . He knew that something bad had happened further down the estate. He just KNEW it.

Janice was fussing around Reggie's body. 'Leave it. Don't touch it. Forensics are on their way and they don't want the body tampered with,' Dave barked. Janice stopped what she was doing and was beckoned over by Jed and Carl. The three of them comforted each other as Janice started sobbing.

Dave cursed as he tried again to ring Heather. He finally got through. 'What's happened?' he said loudly. He stood there as the energy drained away from him. His voice turned into a whisper. The horror that he was feeling was astounding. The phone call finished, Dave held the phone to his chest and looked at the dead butler.

'What?' asked Carl. The three colleagues held their breath, dreading what Dave was about to tell them.

'Sir Hugh's friend, Clive Villiers, has also been shot dead' said Dave. The shock of recent events had knocked the stuffing out of the four of them. No one uttered a word. They just stood there with glazed looks on their faces.

Dave eventually shook himself back into professionalism. 'Okay, guys, I need a bed sheet out here, please.' Jed, Carl and Janice left. He took his phone out of his pocket and dialled his boss. The phone rang and he waited, then the phone cut to voicemail. 'Sir, ring me back as soon as possible, please.' He clicked the phone off and wandered over to the body, wondering how on earth two people could be killed on his watch. 'Oh my God!' he mumbled to himself.

The trio of workers returned with Jed carrying a sheet while Carl walked with his arm around Janice's shoulder in an attempt at comfort.

Dave's phone rang and he answered it. 'Sir, dreadful news. There's been a double shooting at the Bane-Everidge Estate.'

'Are you serious?' Peter nearly blew Dave's ears off then continued his rant, 'There's four CIDs down there and there's been two shootings...' The pause seemed to last forever. 'This is unbelievable! Do what you can. I will alert all and sundry that the place is going into lockdown. No one goes anywhere. Get everyone accounted for. Get everyone in the same goddamn room and get all their mobile phones. Make sure that absolutely none of this is leaked to the press. I'm on my way. I might as well notify the flaming army. Jeez!' The phone clicked off.

Dave said to the three members of staff, 'We need everybody in the lounge now. Jed, if anyone is in the kitchen or the laundrette, can you round them up and take them to the lounge.'

'Yeah, okay. I'll do that. You know what you police are ... all useless. Four people have all been shot dead. Two today while you've been down here investigating,' said Jed, starting to get angry.

Janice intervened, 'Not now, Jed. It's bad enough. Leave it.' Jed stood there rigid and tense. 'Pleeeaaaassse, Jed,' Janice pleaded then started sobbing. 'Don't make matters worse,' she said through her tears then let out a big wail. It was pitiful.

The anger seemed to evaporate from Jed. 'Okay, I'll go and find the rest of the staff.'

Dave accompanied Carl and Janice on the walk towards the lounge. They went inside and he rang Claire. 'Everyone needs to be in the lounge, pronto. DI Thompson is on his way with the Eighth Army.'

Clare then instructed everyone on the patio that they all had to make their way to the lounge. The distant but distinct sound of a helicopter drew Heather's attention. Spyros said to Heather and Claire that he would go and greet the helicopter team and bring them in.

Gina stood staring at the body, transfixed. 'Come on,' said Claire and held out a hand. Gina kept her arms folded and reluctantly started walking with the rest of the group through the dining room towards the lounge. Mary came to assist and put her arm around Gina's shoulder. She then spoke softly to her, 'The detectives have said that forensics are on their way. There's nothing more we could do, Gina. I know it's absolutely awful but we did our best.'

*

Essence of Deceit by Mark Hall

The noise of the helicopter was loud and getting louder as it circled the house in an attempt to land in a suitable place. It landed on the huge lawn in front of the house. Spyros walked swiftly towards the helicopter, its large blades slowly coming to a halt. A team of five climbed out, each man carrying an automatic rifle. Mark Walters was the firearms commanding officer and he shook hands with Spyros. Spyros was big muscled, but Mark was the next level, huge. 'It's like the Wild West here, isn't it?' were Mark's opening words.

'You're not wrong there,' replied Spyros.

'Okay, lads,' said Mark. 'You two go to the left, right up the top and come around the back, and you two go to the right. You should meet round the back somewhere. Keep me informed. Okay, off you go.'

Spyros and Mark exchanged routine professional chit-chat as they made their way to the house. 'Some gaff this is … Phew!' admired Mark. 'I wouldn't like his heating bill in the winter though. It must be enormous.'

'I guess it must be,' added Spyros.

The pair climbed the steps up to the large main front door and Spyros knocked loudly. The door was answered by Heather.

Spyros did a brief introduction then the three of them walked to the lounge.

The lounge had filled up with the Bane-Everidge staff. They were ashen faced and shocked. Dave spoke with Mark. They knew each other reasonably well. Dave indicated to Mark to open up the proceedings. The four detectives stood back.

Dave whispered to Spyros, 'Give him plenty of room. He's massive. Four Weetabix that one.' Heather heard Dave and let out a discreet giggle.

Mark stood in front of the staff, who were mostly sitting down on chairs they'd got from the dining room or from the stack at the back of the lounge. He introduced himself then got down to business.

Dave's phone rang and he quickly and discreetly dealt with the call. He quietly told Spyros to go and let the boss and Fergus in. Spyros left the room.

Mark continued after brief pause, 'We have four armed officers patrolling the grounds. More armed police are on their way, as well as uniformed officers. They'll be here very shortly.' Peter and Fergus politely eased round the door into the lounge so as not to be a distraction. Mark carried on, 'We will find and apprehend this lunatic.' He clapped the palm of his hand with his fist to emphasise his intention.

'Oh, I don't think it's a lunatic, far from it. I think it's an assassin trying to bump us off one by one,' Jed shouted. With that, murmurings and noise filled the room.

'Okay, quiet please,' instructed Dave. He then looked around the room. 'Is everybody here?'

Sir Hugh groaned, 'Archie Sangster, the gardener, isn't here and Phil Atkins from the kitchen isn't here either.'

Janice stepped forwards and counted the staff, giving their names to the detectives. She felt responsible for the members of staff and fussed around them like a mother hen. She mentioned Sir Hugh last and when she mentioned him she looked very uneasy. Heather noticed this and was curious. Was it the wrong protocol? the stress and shock of events? she wondered, but the thought was instantly forgotten when the doors to the lounge were flung open and Archie and Phil came walking awkwardly in. Phil was still in his kitchen whites and blue apron and had his arm under Archie's armpit.

Carl and Mary arranged a chair for Archie. 'I think he's been hit,' said Phil as the three of them wrestled Archie into the chair. Peter wanted to get on and did extremely well to hide his annoyance.

Sir Hugh made a comment. 'He's probably drunk again.' He shook his head and turned towards Janice. 'If he wasn't so good at his job, I'd have got rid of him ages ago.'

Mark indicated to Peter that he'd said his piece and wanted to get to his team in the grounds of the house. He left the room. Archie groaned in his chair, but no one took any notice.

Peter then addressed everyone in the room. 'Because of the gravity of this situation, you are in lockdown. No one leaves. There will be no visitors and no food or provisions will be brought in.' Archie put his hand up gingerly.

'Yes, what is it?' asked Peter.

'My head hurts,' was the feeble reply.

This time, Peter's annoyance was visible. 'Could one of you get him a wet cloth or something.'

'I'll go,' said Mary and she quickly made her way out of the lounge.

'As I was saying,' Peter continued, 'this lockdown is for your own safety.'

Jed started to make a comment, but Janice shot him a shut the hell up look. There was a look of bewilderment and discontent on the faces of the staff in response to Peter's new rules and restrictions.

'It's like a war zone,' Janice whispered in Gina's ear.

Peter carried on, 'Forensics will be here very shortly and more armed police and uniformed officers are also on their way. You'll all be interviewed individually.'

Mary crept back in and passed a wet cloth to Archie as discreetly as possible, which he put on his forehead. Mary pulled an unsympathetic face as she walked over to join Janice, Sir Hugh and Gina who were standing at the side of the lounge. 'There's nothing wrong with him. Useless lump,' she whispered to Gina.

'Everything alright now?' asked Peter with a touch of sarcasm. 'You can go about your daily business within the confines of the estate and house. Just to repeat, we will speak to you all again one by one very shortly. If you have any information at all, if you have seen anything or heard anything, if a colleague's behaviour is different or something is not normal, then come and speak to one of the detectives. You'll be treated with the utmost confidentiality and discretion.' Heather went out the room then came back in again with a briefcase, which she opened up on a small table.

Peter addressed the staff again. 'On your way out, please can you all give your mobile phones to DC Barnes. Thank you, that'll be all for the moment.'

There was a chorus of voices saying that they hadn't got their phones, that they'd left them in the living quarters. There was a bit of a din, with raised voices and chairs being moved.

Peter barked across the noise, 'Okay, listen please. If you haven't got your mobiles with you, can you please go and get them now.' Some of the staff left. Heather started to put mobile phones in separate plastic bags with the owner's name written on a paper tag.

The detectives were standing together when Sir Hugh walked over. He spoke to Peter.

'How can we go about our daily business like this and what's going to happen to the bodies?'

Peter was struck by the complete lack of sympathy and understanding shown by Sir Hugh. 'This is extremely difficult for everybody concerned, Sir Hugh. Forensics will be here in the next few minutes and they'll do their bit. Then the bodies will be taken away. This is an unprecedented and unique situation that we're in. My team and I are doing our absolute best. Please ensure that you and your staff also do your best to cooperate with us.'

'Fine,' responded Sir Hugh quietly. 'I'll go and get my mobile.'

As Sir Hugh walked away, Fergus said to Peter, 'He's disgusting.'

Peter spoke to his team. 'There's no time like the present. We'll question a few of the staff members now.'

Christine from forensics and Sergeant Hoskins came in together. Peter took them to one side and gave them a brief run down of events. Sergeant Hoskins told them how many more uniformed police and armed police had arrived at the house. Christine and Sergeant Hoskins then left to get on with the job in hand.

Staff started to come back in with their mobile phones and hand them over and the lounge got busy again. Heather was bagging up Archie's mobile phone when Dave came over. 'Okay, Mr Sangster. Let's move out the way a bit. I'll get a couple of chairs and we'll have a quick chat.'

Peter asked Heather for an update on the mobile phones.

'I have phones from Janice Brown, Mary Edmunds, Gina Fitzsimmons, Carl Watts, Phil Atkins, Archie Sangster and Diego Garcia. I don't have Jed Mullins' phone yet, or Sir Hugh's,' she said.

'Okay, Heather, thanks. We'll use them now when we're questioning them but then we'll hand them over to forensics and they can have a really deep dig.'

Peter called the rest of his team over and started issuing instructions. 'Claire, grab Archie Sangster's mobile from Heather. Go over to Dave and have a look through it. Archie is around the grounds twenty-four seven. See if you can get something out of him. Spyros, you go join them as well. I'll go to the study with Fergus and Heather. We'll question Sir Hugh, Jed Mullins, Phil Atkins and Diego Garcia. Also, Janice Brown, Mary Edmunds, Gina Fitzsimmons and Carl Watts will need speaking to as well. Good luck team.'

Claire and Spyros approached Dave and Archie. Dave was questioning Archie. Claire started to scroll through the mobile.

'So, Mr Sangster,' said Dave.

'Call me Archie. I don't mind,' interjected the gardener.

Essence of Deceit by Mark Hall

'Well, Archie, you told us that when Reggie Milner and Clive Villiers were shot, you were around the back repairing the greenhouses.'

'Yes, that's right. A couple of panes had broken and some of the wood frames were not too good. They needed replacing. There's always something to do. I'm always busy.'

'How's it going with the phone?' whispered Spyros to Claire.

'Mm, so-so,' was her reply. She continued scrolling through the mobile then blew out a sigh. 'There's nothing on here. Only a few texts from Sir Hugh … job instructions basically. It looks like Archie hardly ever used it. He seems to be a bit of a loner. If there's anything of interest, we'll certainly find it out.'

'What we need to know, Archie, is whether you've seen anything suspicious, anything unusual?' continued Dave.

Spyros joined in the questioning. He was sceptical about Archie's supposedly sore head and asked, 'How are you feeling, Archie? How's your head?'

'Okay,' responded Archie. He rubbed the right side of his head slowly.

'You like a bit of a drink, don't you, Archie?' Spyros pressed.

'Well, yeah, now and again.'

Dave leaned forwards. 'I've been led to believe that it's a bit more than now and again. Were you drunk, Archie? Or did the assassin give you a whack round the head, eh?'

'I don't know,' replied Archie. 'I might've bent down and banged my head on one of the frames.' The detectives came to the conclusion that he was drunk and that this wasn't worth pursuing anymore.

'Archie, as the gardener, you're around the grounds all the time…'

'I'm not just a gardener. Sir Hugh says that I'm very valuable because I can repair all sorts of things. I can do carpentry, bricklaying and concreting.'

'Yes, Archie, we get the picture. You're very valuable but you see all the grounds. To repeat the question, you're outside a lot of the time. Have you seen anything unusual or anything different?'

Archie pulled a face of concentration. 'Nope, nothing,' he replied.

Dave pursued the questioning. 'But, Archie, four people have been shot on this estate.'

There was a long pause. 'I ain't seen nothing, nothing at all. I'm sorry I can't help.' Archie bowed his head and wept quietly.

Dave squeezed Archie's hand gently and said, 'Ok, Archie, we understand. It's a horrible time. Thank you for helping us.'

'Can I go now?' Archie asked.

'Yes, you can, for the time being.' Archie stood up and walked away.

Spyros made the last comment. 'Eyes and ears, Archie, eyes and ears.'

As he left the room, Archie held the door open for Christine. She came over to Dave. 'My team are tending to both bodies at present,' Christine stated.

'The boss is in the study with Heather,' Dave stated.

'Okay, fine. I'll update him. There's more police and the dog squad have just turned up.'

'Spyros, take Christine to the study to see DI Thompson. The boss might want you down there as he'll probably go outside with Christine. I don't know for sure, but go and check.'

'Okay, Dave, will do.'

Essence of Deceit by Mark Hall

Spyros and Christine headed towards the study. Spyros tapped on the door. 'Come,' they heard so they entered the room. Fergus and Heather were sorting through the mobile phones.

Peter greeted Christine then looked at his watch. 'I'm waiting for Sir Hugh. How did it go with Archie Sangster, Spyros?'

'Blankety blank, basically.'

Peter grunted. 'This place is full of see no evil, hear no evil and speak no evil but we'll get to the bottom of this, mark my words. Okay, Spyros, carry on and check back with me later.'

Spyros acknowledged with a 'Sir' and left the study. Peter turned his attention to Christine. 'We have the mobile phones now so that's another job for your team.'

'My team are with both bodies.'

'Okay, let's go,' said Peter. They walked briskly from the lounge, through the reception area to the front door, down the steps and onto the gravel drive.

Sergeant Hoskins came over. 'I have ten officers with me. Another four armed officers and two police dogs. We're working with Mark Walters and his team. We'll fine-tooth comb this place. You can be sure of that.'

'I hope forensics conjure up a bit of magic. We certainly need all the help we can get,' added Peter just as his phone rang. It was Fergus letting him know that Sir Hugh had arrived. 'Ok, on my way.' He turned to Christine and said he had to go back to the study.

'No problem. Forensics will deal with the bodies and update you. Good luck with Sir Hugh,' said Christine.

'Thanks, I'll need it,' replied Peter. The pair turned on their heels and parted, back to the business of what they had to do. Peter wanted to see Dave in the lounge before joining Fergus and Heather with their "chat" with Sir Hugh.

Dave, Claire and Spyros acknowledged their boss as he walked into the lounge.

'Okay, I see you're just about speak to Janice. I won't hold you up. There's been nothing from Archie Sangster, I understand?' said Peter.

Spyros passed Janice's mobile phone to Dave, who looked up from his chair. 'Not a thing. Not an iota.'

Peter huffed, 'Okay, I'll leave you to it and catch up with you later.' He left the room.

Dave started questioning Janice. 'Let's start from when you left the interview you had with my CID officers earlier.'

'Er, I went back to the living quarters to get my cigarettes and I bumped into Reggie. We had a bit of a chat.'

Dave was scrolling through her phone then stopped and looked closer at the screen. 'Carry on, Janice. What happened next?'

'I had another cigarette,' she replied.

'Yes, then what, Janice?' Dave asked.

'Oh, I went back to the house.'

'Why, Janice?'

'To get back to work, to do the usual stuff. There's always plenty to do,' she explained.

'Oh, I see,' replied Dave, feeling he was onto something. 'Let me remind you, Janice, that you got a phone call.'

'Did I?'

'Yes, you did. Who was it from?'

'Yes, I remember now. It was from Sir Hugh.'

Dave kept pushing with the questions. 'Your mobile phone received the call at four-forty-five, which was around the time of the shootings. They happened between four-forty-five and about five-fifteen or five-thirty. What do you say, Janice? It was a handy time to get a phone call and leave Reggie Milner isolated, eh? Was it a window of opportunity for the assassin, Janice, or just coincidence and good timing by Sir Hugh?'

Janice went pale. 'I don't know,' she said and put her head in her hands. 'Look, I really don't know. I got the phone call, that's all. I don't know anything about what you're saying or suggesting. I've done nothing wrong, nothing wrong...' She stopped.

'Please carry on,' Claire prompted.' I know it's difficult.'

'I was heading back towards the house then I heard Jed shouting. He sounded extremely distressed so I ran back to where the noise was coming from. Carl was there too. Then I looked and I could see Reggie flat on the ground.' She drifted off and stared at the carpet. 'It was where we'd had a fag and a chat. A few minutes later you turned up.'

'Okay, thank you, Janice.' The four of them sat there for a moment in silence then Dave looked at Spyros and Claire with as expression of job done, no more questions. Claire whispered, 'Yeah, fine,' and Spyros nodded in agreement.

'You can go now, Janice,' said Dave. 'I'm sure we'll speak again. Thanks for your time.' Janice said thanks then got up and left.

*

In the study, the team of detectives led by Peter were in the process of questioning Sir Hugh.

'How convenient that you've erased everything on your phone. Have you got something to hide? Don't worry, forensics will help us out on this one.' Peter paused to let that sink in.

Sir Hugh responded, 'I always clear my phone. It's a habit. Nothing more and nothing less.'

There was a knock and Dave walked in. 'Sir, just a quick update.'

Peter indicated to Fergus to carry on the interview. 'What have you got, Dave?' he asked.

'The Janice Brown interview was interesting…'

Peter and Dave moved away from the others to discuss what went on during the interview.

Glaswegian detective, Fergus, took up the questioning with Sir Hugh. 'Sir Hugh, we've had a double shooting. Reggie Milner was shot at the far end of the house and Clive Villiers was shot on the patio. He was waiting for you, drinking gin and tonic. What was the delay, Sir Hugh? Why did you leave your friend all alone, eh?'

Heather could sense the utter contempt that Sir Hugh had for Fergus. She hoped that Fergus wouldn't pick up on it, otherwise all hell would break loose. Although Fergus was a total professional, he had a very short fuse. DI Thompson said it was down to Scottish air and whisky.

Sir Hugh eventually answered, 'I was on the phone.'

'Who to?' asked Fergus. Sir Hugh took his time answering. 'Don't worry, Sir Hugh. If you can't remember, we'll find out.'

'I was speaking to a government official,' Sir Hugh replied matter-of-factly.

Peter finished speaking with Dave, who left. He listened quietly for a moment before sitting back down beside Fergus and picking up the thread of the interview. 'Sir Hugh, during these last two shootings, I put it to you that you were on the phone each time. The call to Janice Brown isolated Reggie Milner so that the assassin had a clear target. During the second call, Clive Villiers was left alone on the patio.'

'Absolute total rubbish!' gasped Sir Hugh. 'This is so ridiculous as to be unbelievable. You think I had my close friend, Clive Villiers, shot as well as my butler? This is absolutely madness. You are all a bunch of retards.' Sir Hugh got to his feet, seething. 'I'm not speaking to you lot anymore. Not until I get my lawyer.'

'Oh, dear, Sir Hugh. We are in a tizz.' Peter's voice was slow and clear.

'I'll get another lawyer,' barked Sir Hugh.

'Fine, Sir Hugh, that's fine. We're going to wrap up now. Make sure you get a good night's sleep. My team will be back tomorrow and we'll want to question everyone. In the meantime, you'll have twenty-four-hour police protection outside with no coming or going of your staff, but you know that anyway. I believe forensics are still outside.' Peter indicated to Heather. 'Go and tell Dave and the others to wrap up as soon as they can. Tell everyone to get to the office at eight am sharp, then we'll come back down here.'

The team of detectives left the building. Peter was doing a walk and talk with Fergus. 'I'll have a word with Sergeant Hoskins and forensics and see what's happening.'

Essence of Deceit by Mark Hall

Fergus replied, 'Okay, sir. Do you want me to catch Mark Walters?'

'No, that's fine, Sergeant Hoskins can deal with that.'

In the grounds of the house it was busy, with police officers moving to and fro. Peter caught the attention of an officer and asked whether Sergeant Hoskins about.

'I'll radio him,' said the officer and got Sergeant Hoskins on the radio. 'Sergeant Hoskins, DI Thompson wants an update.' He gave the radio to Peter.

Sergeant Hoskins replied, 'I'm with forensics at the moment, with Reggie Milner. The bullet found in Reggie Milner is the same as the one in Clive Villiers on the patio. They were both headshots. Very accurate.'

Peter sighed. 'What about the police sweep? Fine-tooth combing? Any luck? And has Mark Walters found anything?'

'Nothing as yet,' replied Sergeant Hoskins. 'Walters is going to take a real good look all around the boundaries and beyond. And as you know we've got the dogs too.'

'Okay, keep me posted.' Peter clicked off the radio and handed it back to the officer. The rest of his team had congregated at the bottom of the main steps and he joined them. 'We still have to speak to Gina Fitzsimmons, Carl Watts and the others. We also need to get a bit more out of Janice Brown. We got nothing from Archie Sangster and Sir Hugh had a hissy fit.'

'I heard about that,' Dave added. 'Did you not warn him, sir?'

Peter allowed himself a big grin. 'If we give him enough rope, who knows? Perhaps, he may hang himself. See you in the morning.'

The team climbed into two four-by-fours. Dave drove one, with Claire and Spyros as passengers. In the other vehicle were Peter, Heather and Fergus. The cars travelled down the long driveway at speed. The summer evening was drawing to a close. The noise of a helicopter filled the night sky, with searchlights beaming across the Bane-Everidge Estate.

Dave dropped Claire and Spyros off at their abodes. Peter dropped off Heather at her house then drove to Fergus' house, although he lived a touch further away from headquarters than the rest.

Essence of Deceit by Mark Hall

Fergus wasn't paying much attention to the journey. He was looking at his phone for the next day's horse racing, He realised where they were. 'Hey, sir, you could have dropped me off at HQ. My car's there.'

Peter looked at Fergus. 'I thought I was doing you a favour. You'll have to get the train in tomorrow.'

Fergus huffed, 'No worries, sir. It'll be fine. You gonna come in for a wee dram?'

'Not really, Fergus, but thanks for the offer. I'm still on duty.'

'Boss, you're not on duty now!' Peter gave him a half friend, half boss look and Fergus knew it was time to withdraw. He thought to himself that the boss was always on duty, twenty-four seven. He got out of the car. 'See you in the morning, boss.'

'Okay, Fergus.'

'Sure you won't come in for a quick one?'

'No thanks.' Fergus gave a mock salute and walked up the path.

Peter soon rocked up at his home, turned into the drive and turned the engine off. He started to wonder if he'd pulled the team too early but the gun squad was there as well as Sergeant Hoskins and his boys. Forensics were still there too. He blew through his teeth. Nah, he'd made the right decision. He had to keep the troops fresh.

He climbed out his vehicle, opened the boot to check that the work stuff, such as folders, was all there in order and that the mobiles bagged up by Heather were labelled. He slammed the boot shut and walked towards the house. Kay's red and black Mini turned into the drive.

Peter waited at the front door for her. Kay got out of the Mini and slammed the door. 'You're out late, Kay. It's eleven-forty.'

'Yeah, I went to the gym and sauna with Rachel and then back to hers for coffee,' said Kay.

Peter opened the front door and they both headed straight to the kitchen and flung their coats on chairs. Peter filled the kettle. 'Do you want another coffee, Kay? Although it seems that you not long had one.'

'No, I'll have hot water. No more caffeine. You hungry, Peter?'

'Not a great deal. I'll do myself beans on toast.'

'How's it going down at massacre house?' Kay enquired.

'It's hell. Complete madness. There were two people shot dead today, the butler and a friend of Sir Hugh's, within minutes of each other.'

'Are you any nearer to catching the killer? Any clues yet?' Kay asked.

'We're pretty certain that the killer is an assassin. He's like a ghost. He leaves no trace, nothing. Four people have been shot dead. All headshots and very accurate. One shot was through the back window of the limo from about seventy yards.'

'Wow, that's some hot shot! So you have no leads, no idea?' Kay mused.

Peter took a sip of coffee and put two slices of bread in the toaster. He went to the cupboard that housed the tinned food and searched for some baked beans. He then mumbled, 'Beans, where's the beans?'

'They're in there,' said Kay. She moved along the worktop to allow her husband more space.

Peter grabbed a tin then stopped. He'd noticed something on the side of his wife's face. He moved closer. 'What are those scratches there?' he said, looking closer and touching his wife gently. 'How did you get these? Have you looked in a mirror, Kay?'

'No, it's nothing,' replied Kay.

'The scratches go from your eyebrow down to the top of your cheek,' Peter pointed out.

'Look, it really is nothing. Please stop touching my face.' She was getting irritated. 'If you really want to know, I did it at work. I was moving some roses on to a top shelf. I was on an awkward stepladder and trying to push them up and I got scratched. Okay, happy now?'

Peter kept staring at Kay. 'Really, is that what happened?'

'Oh, leave it out, Peter. You're always the detective. Never off duty. Give it a rest, I'm off to bed.' As she hurried out of the kitchen, she turned around and said to her husband, 'You've burnt your toast.'

Peter had a fitful night's sleep. In the morning, the alarm and his phone went off at the same time. He picked up his phone and left the alarm beeping. Kay shouted at him to turn it off, for Christ's sake. It was Christine on the phone.

Essence of Deceit by Mark Hall

'Hold on, hold on,' Peter replied. He silenced the alarm then grabbed his trousers and headed for the bathroom. 'What's happening?'

'Reggie Milner was shot in the back of the head. The assassin was probably hiding in the bushes on the perimeter of the grounds and then went around to the other side of the house and shot Clive Villiers in the side of the head not long afterwards. Whether that was planned or chance who knows? As with all the shootings, there's been no trace of anything apart from an earring. Well, it's more of a gold stud … quite nice actually. It was found by the hedge that runs alongside the swimming pool. Our team's assumption is that the assassin had a good view of the patio area and hid in the hedge. But whether the earring belongs to the assassin or somebody else we'll have to check. I'll see you at HQ. Then we can go through it all.'

'Okay, fine,' replied Peter and clicked his phone off.

He showered, got dressed and went downstairs to have coffee and toast with marmalade, not burnt this time. Kay came into the kitchen, dressed smart casual, ready for the day at the florists.

Peter was drawn to the scratches on Kay's face. He couldn't help himself. Kay was buttering her toast and she slammed the knife down. 'What?'

'Oh, nothing.' He hesitated. 'Those scratches don't look so bad now.'

'Make up,' was his wife's terse reply.

Peter drove into the office car park. Other members of the CID team were also turning up. He parked then waited for Claire at the back entrance of the building. The pair walked together. Peter held the door open.

Claire took some of Peter's office stuff. 'How are you today, sir?' she enquired.

'Yep, alright, not too bad. And how are you, Claire?'

'Okay, sir, thanks.'

The team assembled in the office. Peter went to the incident board, which was basically divided into three columns with 'Victims', 'Suspects', and a big question mark that meant people of interest. He looked at the victims then wrote, 'number 3, Reggie Milner (butler)'. He also added, 'number 4, Clive Villiers (friend of Sir Hugh)'. He tidied up the board so it was bang up to date.

Essence of Deceit by Mark Hall

Peter looked at the board and took a moment. He looked at 'Gary Hinchcliffe, chauffeur number 1' and wrote that down on a notepad. He also wrote down 'Diego Garcia, chauffeur number 2'. He went back to the board and looked at the words 'Assassin – self-motivated or hired?' He didn't say a word but tapped the board with his felt pen.

'Dave, can you take Claire and Spyros to the house and question Mary Edmunds, Gina Fitzsimmons, Carl Watts, Jed Mullins, Phil Atkins and Diego Garcia. Heather, try to find something on the first chauffeur, Gary Hinchcliffe, here in the office.'

The team got ready to do their various assignments. There was a knock at the door and Christine entered the office. All heads and eyes turned towards her and she didn't waste any time. 'I spoke to DI Thompson earlier, but the assassin shot Reggie Milner in the back of the head from a distance. He must have been on the edge of the field hidden by the trees. But, the remarkable thing is that the assassin moved down past the kitchen, sleeping quarters and bin area and past the greenhouses to the back of the swimming pool. It's very likely that the assassin then moved along the side of the pool and hid in the long hedge. He had a perfect view of the patio and house. He executed Clive Villiers then disappeared, evaporated, in fact.'

Peter made a comment. 'No one saw a thing. There were four CID officers and no one saw a goddamn thing!' He was furious. 'What the hell were you lot doing? Jeeeezzz!' He ran his hand through his hair. Dave put his hand to his face and Heather bit her lip. Claire glared at Spyros who looked very uncomfortable.

Christine continued. She held up a clear plastic bag. 'A gold stud earring was found by the hedge bordering the pool. Who it belongs to we don't know, but it was found in an area where we suspect this assassin was operating.' She passed the bag to Peter.

He looked at it closely and a feeling of dread came over him. He looked even closer and the feelings got worse. Although he remained cold and professional on the outside, inside emotional turmoil warred with police logic and reason. He passed the bag to Dave, still processing his thoughts. It looked like one of Kay's earrings. It couldn't be. Plenty of women wore them, surely? He came back to the present.

'What's up with you Spyros?' asked Fergus.' You not seen a woman's earring before?' But Peter had.

Spyros was holding the bag now and there was no hiding his body language. He had an awful feeling who the earring belonged to. It could be one of Kay's, the governor's missus. He passed the bag to Claire and blew his nose on a tissue, trying to hide his body language and compose himself. Both Fergus and Peter were looking at Spyros. He felt like he was under a spotlight. If in doubt, bullshit. 'One of my ex-girlfriend's had a pair like that back home in Cyprus. It just brought back memories, that's all.'

'Happy ones?' enquired Fergus.

'Yeah, good, very good.' Spyros regained control of himself. Obviously, Fergus had bought it but Peter still had doubts. He didn't know what to think.

Christine took back the plastic bag. 'This is all we have to go on at the moment. We will check this ear stud for DNA. Also, we're going through the mobile phones. Hopefully, we'll get something to go on.' Peter thanked her and she left the office.

Peter addressed his team. 'Okay, everyone. You all know where we're at. Let's go.' He nodded to Dave. 'Good luck. Keep me posted.'

Dave replied with the usual protocol, 'Sir.'

Peter looked at his watch. 'I reckon that Sergeant Hoskins will be nearly finishing shifts. Fergus, can you ring him, please, and, Heather, please ring Mark Walters.'

The team got cracking. Peter went to the water cooler then to his private office.

He sat down at his desk and checked his computer for any new emails. None had come in. He stared at the old taunting email and read it again:

How very unfortunate that you lost the case when more compelling evidence was staring you in the face. If you had looked hard enough instead of being blind, the guilty would be locked up doing time. Justice will be served. It won't be long. Very soon the guilty will be gone.

He stared at it, willing a clue to come out. Why had they got these emails? What was going on in this person's mind? There were four dead. Were there going to be any more? he wondered. Why these four? Roland Van Mendes, Reggie Milner and Clive Villiers were all close to Sir Hugh. Why not Sir Hugh? And why the chef, Ben Charles? He smirked, recalling Fergus' comment about shite food.

Essence of Deceit by Mark Hall

Peter picked up the office phone and called the forensics' tech boys. The phone was answered. 'Hi, is that Eugene?'

'Speaking.'

'Is there any news on tracing these emails?' enquired Peter.

'No, not yet, sir,' said Eugene. 'We're still working on it. It's quite a tough nut to crack.'

'The story of my life at the moment. We keep on running up dead ends. Christine will have some mobile phones for you to look at from the Bane-Everidge Estate. Okay, Eugene, catch you later. Keep at it.'

'Okay, sir, will do.'

Peter sat back in his chair and his brain started to churn, thinking about Kay. The earring had looked familiar. He exhaled loudly. The scratches on her face. Were they from hiding in the bushes? He didn't know, but she was definitely a hot shot. There was no doubt about that and she did think that the police were all incompetent, always thinking she could do better. But would she really have done this? She didn't talk much about her time in the force. Did she still hold resentment? Surely not.

He started to sweat, the dread creeping in like fog rolling in from the sea, darkening everything, consuming, suffocating. A rap at the door broke the gloom. Peter stood up, trying to get into boss mode. 'What have you got, Heather?' Heather answered and started to update him. He wasn't listening. He decided that he needed to investigate Kay with the most extreme secretness he could muster.

'Sir, I said that Mark Walters has left the house. He's done a thorough search and given a report to Sergeant Hoskins,' said Heather.

Peter interrupted, 'Don't tell me. He's found zilch.'

'Well, yes, you're right, sir.'

Peter twiddled a pencil between his fingers. Heather stood with her hands on her hips. 'So, all that's been found is an ear stud,' he remarked. 'Can you have a look into the so-called retirement of Gary Hinchcliffe?'

'Ok, sir. Will do.'

*

The CID team of three were on their way to the Bane-Everidge Estate. Dave was driving the white Volvo four-by-four accompanied by Claire and Spyros. Dave and Claire were in the front, making small talk about rugby. Whenever Dave was off duty, or had the chance, he went to watch the Wasps rugby team. Claire went occasionally with an old flame. She enjoyed it but couldn't get the gist of it.

In the back, Spyros had no time for small talk. He had to deal with his inner turmoil. He gazed out of the window and replayed in his head what had happened.

Right, so he'd had a coffee with Kay at Mandell's Health Club. She'd been for a swim and a sauna after work. He'd been to the gym. They accidentally on purpose bumped into each other in the cafeteria. They'd had an on-and-off affair some time ago. They were both married and very discreet about it. They'd decided to put the block on it when there'd been whisperings in the office, but the fire hadn't completely gone out. There was always a spark if they happened to bump into each other.

Spyros continued to analyse what had gone on. He'd spilt his coffee and gone to the counter to grab a cloth and a couple of paper towels. It was only a minor spill. Kay had been busy texting on her mobile. He'd sat down and Kay had put her phone down. She'd fiddled with her ear studs and said that they were irritating. She'd put the studs on the table and wiped her ears gently with a towel from her bag. Her phone had rung and Kay had stood up, mobile to her ear. She'd taken a quick gulp of coffee, said bye and dashed off, forgetting her ear studs. They'd been left on the table. It must have been an important call.

He'd drunk his coffee and put the ear studs in his trouser pocket. He'd had on his dark green trousers at the time. The following day, he'd been going to nip into the florists where Kay worked. That'd been the day they were at the Bane-Everidge Estate and he'd gone for a swim in the pool. The earrings must have fallen out in the mad rush.

Spyros weighed up his options. If the earring wasn't Kay's, then he was in the clear. If it was, then what should he say?

'Spyros, we're going to interview the remaining staff in the study, alright?' said Dave, jolting Spyros back to the present.

'Suits me, whatever,' replied Spyros.

The car turned into the long drive. The helicopter had gone and a couple of armed police walked across the field. Dave lowered the window on Claire's side, slowed the car down then stopped.

'How's it going?' asked Dave. 'Is it just you two armed boys?'

'No, the other two are around the back. The helicopter went back with Mark Walters. I don't know how much longer we're here for. There's supposed to be a shift change.'

'What's new?' enquired Dave.

'Nothing really,' came the reply. 'Forensics have taken the bodies away. They've been very busy. But having said that, nothing's been found, although we heard that an earring was found, but that could be anybody's, I suppose.'

'Okay, thanks a lot.' Dave elevated the window.

Spyros commented, 'It looks like those two of Walters are never out of the gym by the size of them.'

'Yeah, they're big sods,' commented Dave. The car sped up to the house.

'Here we are, the Mansion of Doom!' declared Spyros.

Dave parked the car and the three detectives climbed out of the vehicle. As they did so, Sergeant Hoskins came round the corner. 'We've fine-tooth combed everywhere again. We had a couple of dogs too. Walters did a big sweep through with the helicopter with infrared search lights but there was nothing. The only thing that was found was a gold stud earring, but I guess you know that anyway. It's really strange. Not even the dogs have picked anything up. It's baffling.' Sergeant Hoskins looked at his watch. 'There's gonna be a shift change very shortly. Sergeant Peters will be here, so there will be uniformed officers and armed boys as well.'

'Good,' replied Dave. 'Okay, Sergeant, leave you to it. Keep in touch.' The three CIDs walked towards the house and up the steps. The door was opened by Gina. Brief greetings were exchanged, then Dave got straight down to business. 'We need to talk to you, Mary, Carl, Jed, Diego and Phil. This will all take place in the study.'

*

Back at HQ, Heather was at her desk and on the search for Gary Hinchcliffe, the first chauffeur. She swivelled round in the chair to talk to Fergus and Peter. 'So he retired. A quiet exit from the Bane-Everidge Estate. No retirement party. He just up and left.'

Fergus expressed his opinion. 'So, Gary Hinchcliffe goes and the Colombian chauffeur, Diego Garcia, rocks up. I reckon he's a drug go-between.'

'Yes, he's a strange one,' injected Peter. 'The Colombian, Diego Garcia, is on the list to be questioned today. It'll be interesting to see what Dave and the guys come up with.'

Heather continued, 'Hinchcliffe's so-called retirement was on the eighth of May, two weeks before the court case, which was on the twenty-second of May. A couple of days later, Diego Garcia comes on board. He started on the eleventh. As we know, he's Colombian, speaks good English and has all the relevant papers. It seems all legit and correct.' The three detectives paused for a moment. Peter cupped his chin with his right hand, left hand under his elbow, quietly contemplating.

Fergus broke the silence. 'I don't like this at all. There's a funny smell about it. No, I'll tell you what, it stinks!'

'We'll keep searching, sir,' said Heather.

'Okay, guys, fine. I'll be in my office. I'll get an update from the Bane-Everidge Estate shortly,' said Peter.

*

In the study at the Bane-Everidge Estate, the team of three were questioning Gina. Dave was standing, leaning on a back of a chair, while the other two CIDs were seated. Gina was also seated, facing them.

Dave opened up proceedings. 'So, Gina, tell me again what happened that evening when we had the two shootings.'

'I was hoovering the stairs and reception area at the time.'

'Did you know that Mr Villiers was on the patio?' asked Dave.

'Yes, I did. I saw him in the reception area. We don't always know who's visiting. People come and go. Some stay over.'

'That's interesting,' Dave replied. 'How long have you worked here, Gina?'

'About four years, I think. Yeah, four years.'

'Who's been here the longest?'

'Janice, I suppose. Ten years, I think. Reggie was also here a long time and Gary Hinchcliffe.'

'Really? Two of the longest-serving members of staff aren't here any more. What about the other members of staff? How long have they been here?'

'I dunno. All different, I suppose. Carl's been here a couple of years and Jed about the same.'

'Give me an estimate, Gina.'

'Five to six years, I guess.'

Dave went on, 'And the shortest?'

'It's got to be Diego.'

'How long do you reckon Diego's been here?' asked Dave.

Gina shrugged her shoulders. 'Six weeks, eight weeks.'

'So, Gina, you heard the commotion from the patio. What did you do?'

'I ran down as quick as I could. I was horrified. I saw blood everywhere. Mr Villiers was flat on his back and Sir Hugh was there.' Gina lowered her head and just gazed into space.

'Go on, Gina,' prompted Dave.

'Mary came running out. We tried our best…' Gina started quietly crying. Claire stood up and walked to a small table which had drinking glasses, jugs and small bottles of water. She brought a glass of water over and gave it to Gina, then put her hand on Gina's shoulder trying her best to comfort her.

Gina took out a small tissue from her pocket, blew her nose gently and tried to carry on. 'Then very shortly after, you two turned up.' She looked at Claire and Spyros.

'Yes, that's right. DC Papadakis and I had gone to question Archie Sangster. We didn't quite get there, did we, DC Papadakis?' Claire glared at Spyros. 'Yes, we heard the disturbance and came running. It was an awful scene to witness.'

There was silence and Spyros felt a pang of guilt.

'Anything else you can think of ?' Dave asked Gina.

'No, I've told you everything I know.'

'Okay, thanks for your cooperation. That will do for now. I'm sure we'll speak again very shortly. You can go now, Gina.' She got up and left. Dave turned to Spyros. 'Spyros, go and find Phil Atkins. He'll probably be in the kitchen.'

'Will do, sir.'

Spyros walked along the corridor. That crazy Claire, he thought. Claire the bloody glare. He'd had a quick dip in the pool and, hell, was he paying for it now. He was going to have to have a word with her to keep her gob shut. He could be right in it with this.

Instead of going to the kitchen, he headed for the pool just in case the other earring was there. He didn't want Kay implicated in this. DI Thompson wouldn't understand about his missus leaving the studs in the health club. He was Mr Suspicious from Trust No One Road.

Spyros reached the swimming pool. He knew he didn't have much time, but he was drawn to the pool like a magnet. They said criminals went back to the scene of crime. Oh, the irony. He looked left and right as he walked along the manicured hedge shielding the pool. Nothing. He kept looking, knowing that time was tight. He guessed forensics or the uniformed boys would have found it. He allowed himself a moment. Yeah, he would check his green trousers when he got home. He'd better find Phil Atkins. He'd go the back way.

Spyros realised he had to get a move on. He went past the back of the swimming pool and saw the gardener attending to the greenhouses. He half waved. Archie responded with a nod. Spyros looked to where the gardener was, about forty foot away from him, then scanned his eyes from the gardener and the swimming pool up to the bin area and the kitchen. The kitchen was about sixty yards away. He weighed it up. The assassin might have had to sneak past the gardener. Well, there'd been that big hedge to hide in plus plenty of trees and bushes on the boundary. He was sure that the assassin had made their escape that way, undetected.

Spyros arrived at the kitchen and banged on the back door. There was no answer. He could hear the din inside. He knocked again and walked in. It was all hustle and bustle, pots and pans clanging, busyness in action. 'Hello? It's DC Papadakis.' No one took any notice. Music was blaring. Robbie Williams was on.

Jed eventually noticed him. He turned the radio down and wiped his hands on his overalls. 'Hello, how can we help?'

'I need to speak to Mr Atkins, please. Is he about?'

'One moment. I'll find him.' Jed turned on his heel and walked around the corner. Janice walked past Spyros and they exchanged greetings.

Phil appeared. 'How can I help, detective?'

'Please can you come to study with me. We need to ask you a few questions.'

'Okay,' Phil replied. The pair walked out of the kitchen and off to the study .

When Spyros and Phil arrived at the study, the door was open and they walked in. Dave indicated to Phil to sit in the empty chair. Claire and Spyros also sat down.

Dave paced the floor. 'Mr Atkins, is it okay if I call you Phil?'

'Yeah, fine.'

'You've been here how long?'

'About two minutes, I think.'

Oh, dear, thought Spyros. Fancy rattling Dave when he was in a bad mood.

'Don't muck me about, Phil. Have you been taking 'I'm a prat' pills this morning? I want your utmost cooperation and if I don't get it you'll be down the nick, son. I'll ask you again. How long have you worked for Sir Hugh?'

Phil blew out of his teeth. 'Four or five years.' He slouched in his seat.

Dave was getting more and more irritated by this individual and went straight in. 'Who would want Roland Van Mendes, Ben Charles, Reggie Milner and Clive Villiers dead?'

Phil sat up. 'I haven't got a clue.'

'How did you get on with Ben Charles?' asked Dave.

'Ben, he was sound. A good bloke.'

'Why do you think he was shot?'

Phil pondered for a moment then blew out through his lips. 'I've no idea,' he said and shrugged his shoulders.

'How well do you know Diego Garcia?' Dave asked.

'Not that well. He ain't been here long. He doesn't say much. He's from Brazil, I think.'

'Columbia actually,' Claire interjected.

Dave continued, 'Do you think that it's unusual to have a chauffeur from Colombia?'

'I haven't really thought about it,' Phil mused.

Claire asked a question. 'Were there many Colombians at the social gatherings that Sir Hugh used to host?'

Phil considered the question before answering. 'There were all sorts of people. I don't know about Colombians. What do they look like?' Dave shot Phil a look. 'Okay, I wouldn't say people from all over the place. Sir Hugh knows lots of people. Everyone wanted to be invited to a Bane-Everidge "soiree".'

'Eh, a what?' asked Spyros.

Claire was keen to offer an explanation. 'A soiree is a gathering in the evening. It's a posh do where they wear smart attire. That means clothes to you, DC Papadakis.'

She was really getting on his nerves, Spyros thought. She wasn't content with being Claire the glare, now she wanted to stick a dig in. No wonder she was single.

Dave either didn't notice Claire's dig or just ignored it. He continued with the questions to Phil. 'Wild parties were they, Phil?'

Phil visibly wriggled in his seat. 'Well, you know. Lots to drink. Plenty of fizz and wine and whisky.'

'And drugs, Phil? Were there plenty of drugs flying around?'

'Oh, I don't know.' Phil's body language was telling a different story, which was picked up by Claire.

Dave kept the questions coming. 'Let's go back to night of the party, Phil.'

'I wasn't there,' Phil blurted out.

'Pardon, Phil. You weren't there? Do you need to rethink that?' Dave was closing in.

'I wasn't there, I tell you. I was in Scotland.'

'If that's your answer, Phil, okay. Whereabouts in Scotland?'

'I was at my Uncle Frank's in Glasgow.'

'And the address in Glasgow is what, Phil?'

'Um, Seventy-seven Blackberry Road, Shawlands.'

'Of course, Phil, if we need to check out your alibi, we'll do so.' Dave noticed that Phil had relaxed. Was he telling the truth or resigned to his fate?

Dave decided to draw the interview to a close. 'Okay, Phil, you can go now, for the time being, anyway.' Phil got up and left.

'Dodgy fella, very dodgy,' Claire stated.

'Yeah, deffo,' added Spyros. 'Who else have we got to question?'

Claire looked at her notebook. 'Mary Edmunds, Carl Watts, Jed Mullins and Diego Garcia.'

Dave's mobile rang. 'Sir, yes, yep, okay, sir. Four more. Okay, got that.' He finished the call and clicked the phone off. 'That was the boss. He said to question Mary, Jed and Carl but leave Diego. Diego's gonna be brought into the station very shortly.'

They interviewed the three members of staff but there was nothing different to all the other staff interviews. Mary's recollection of events was the same as Gina's as regarded Clive Villiers' shooting. Jed's and Carl's accounts about finding Reggie Milner both tallied up.

The fateful night of the party seemed to tally up as well, except for one thing ... Phil Atkins. Mary said she'd seen him briefly at the party. He hadn't been at work for two days, but she was sure she'd seen him at the party. Carl and Jed also said they hadn't seen him for two days. Carl didn't know why. Jed said that Phil had flown to Scotland. Both denied seeing him at the party. Although police and CID had interviewed everyone at the party, they thought they had an extremely good case against Sir Hugh. When he was acquitted, with three missing girls still not accounted for and, of course, the suspicious accident of the young man who died, the sheer disappointment and anger was beyond belief.

Dave, Claire and Spyros pondered Mary's statement again. When she was questioned after the party, she'd said that she hadn't seen Phil. Now she was saying that she had. Claire looked through the notes of the recent interviews and put a big circle around the names of Mary Edmunds and Phil Atkins.

It was now time for the detectives to head back to HQ. The three made their way out the house. They went past Gina and Janice busying around. They got in the car. Dave drove with Claire in the front and Spyros in the back.

Spyros started the discussion. 'Do you know what, going back to the party, I remember Phil Atkins giving a statement that he wasn't about that night. He never mentioned Scotland. He just said he wasn't there. He was truthful when he said he wasn't at work for two days. He's obviously dodgy, like we said before. Not unless Mary's got it wrong. But I'm sure when we turn the heat up and question a few more staff we might get something.'

Dave input, 'We do have a chink of light.'

Spyros was puzzled. 'What do you mean, with four shootings, three girls missing, the accident? What's your thinking?'

'Phil Atkins is hiding something.'

'We can certainly all agree on that one,' added Claire. 'Out of all those people at the house, somebody knows something. I guess we'll have to keep digging.'

'Yeah, I guess so,' Dave mumbled. 'I guess so.'

The team continued their journey in quiet contemplation. Spyros started pondering again the dreaded earring. They eventually arrived at the office. Dave parked up and they walked straight in.

In the office, they exchanged the usual minimal greetings. All attention was on Peter and Christine. Christine had forensics paraphernalia on the desk to the left of the incident board. Peter nodded at Christine to commence. She held up a clear plastic bag. Spyros held his breath and so did Peter. They both held a secret they didn't want to explode. Time stood still for these two detectives.

'As you know, this was found by the swimming pool area next to the large hedge leading up to the patio. It's a gold stud earring and it's been checked for DNA.' The tension that Spyros and Peter felt was almost unbearable. 'And we found nothing, no DNA.'

Spyros struggled not to show his relief. Thank God for that! At least Kay was off the hook. Now all he needed was Claire to keep her gob shut about the dip in the pool.

Peter felt initial relief then a mixture of probables and possibles. He still had a nagging feeling that the ear stud might be Kay's. His mind ran through it again. The scratches on the side of her face. Did she get those from the hedge when she was leaning into it? Did the ear stud come out then? Also, there was her incredible shooting ability with a sniper's rifle, her dislike of injustice and her contempt for the police. Peter had come a long way in the force. He had an incredible eye for small details. Some days it was a blessing, but today it felt like a curse.

Christine continued, 'To be fair, the earring could have been dropped anytime from anybody, a staff member or a partygoer.' She implied that the ear stud didn't have much bearing on recent events. She started to wrap up. 'That's it for now. We've almost completed work on the mobile phones. They'll be with you very soon.'

She then spoke quietly to Peter, 'We still haven't traced those emails. It been very difficult indeed. Well, we'll carry on carrying on.' With that, Christine left the office.

Peter walked to the incident board. 'Did you guys manage to glean any more information from the staff at the Bane-Everidge Estate? I take it everyone has been questioned now, except for Diego?'

Dave gave the answers and information. 'Yes, that's correct, sir. A couple of characters need looking at again. We should turn the heat on them, I would say.' Peter looked hopeful.

Claire joined in, 'Mary Edmunds for starters. Now she seems to think she saw Phil Atkins at the fateful party. When she was originally questioned, she hadn't. As for Atkins himself ... it's a gut feeling, but something isn't right. I can't put a finger on it.'

'Yes, he's a slippery little so-and-so. Yeah, there's something about him, sir,' Spyros commented. Dave nodded in agreement.

Peter wrote on the board under the question mark that meant people of interest. Under the two chauffeurs, he added Mary Edmunds, Phil Atkins and Sir Hugh Bane-Everidge. His wife crossed his mind, but, my God, he thought to himself, he wasn't putting Kay up on the board. He dismissed the thought abruptly. The team knew of the boss's procedure with the board. That a person of interest could soon become a suspect.

He stood back from the board and turned to speak to the team. 'Forensics haven't yet found the source of the emails. We haven't received any more. Also, I wonder whether that's the end of the shootings?'

'I hope so, sir, It's getting like the OK Corral,' Fergus commented.

'It's worse than that already. There was three shot at the OK Corral and we're on four at the moment,' stated Claire.

'Are you sure about that? I thought there was loads killed at the OK Corral?' Fergus replied.

'Apparently not, only three. I watched the film late the other night,' Clare added. Fergus and Spyros glanced at each other and they both rolled their eyes. Peter said, 'Okay guys,' which politely meant get back to the job in hand.

'Well, there still plenty of uniform boys down there.'

Peter and the team dissected and discussed the information they had to date.

*

In the kitchen of the Bane-Everidge Estate, all were busy. Sir Hugh had just had a pre-lunch drink. He was going be eating alone that day. There was to be no visitors and no going out either. Mary was on waitress duty. She made her way through the kitchen. Some of the staff ate their lunch in the side annex, a lovely large tiled area with tasteful oak tables and benches. On the menu was a light lunch being prepared by Carl. Smoked salmon, a selection of salads and new potatoes. It was cleverly prepared with imaginative side dishes. There was always a touch of class at the Bane-Everidge Estate. Carl presented Mary with the tray, which she dutifully put on the ornate food trolley. Everything was five star plus.

As Mary left the kitchen, she caught the eye of Phil. Her blood ran cold, albeit very briefly. She felt as if Phil's eyes had pierced her soul. She hurried along. She walked through the building to Sir Hugh's office. She paused for a moment outside the study. Cold sweat moistened her forehead. She tried to make sense of it all. Why did he look at her like that? Did she imagine it? Perhaps Phil knew that she'd told the detectives that she'd seen him at the party. Maybe they'd told him. He might have been listening at the door. 'Oh, no,' Mary whispered to herself.

Still feeling uncomfortable, Mary pushed on with the job in hand. She got to Sir Hugh's office. The door was slightly open and Mary walked straight in. 'Here we are, Sir Hugh.' She placed the tray on the table as Sir Hugh simultaneously moved some paperwork.

'I'm trying to organise a new butler. It's a proper inconvenience. Reggie was so good. I'll probably have to get another chef as well. This really is a nuisance.' Sir Hugh looked at Mary. 'Are you okay, Mary? You look a bit pale.'

'I'm okay, Sir Hugh, thanks. Just a bit of a headache, that's all.'

'Here, let me pour you a glass of water.' Sir Hugh went to a chunky glass jug, filled with water and a couple of slices of lemon. He passed a glass of water to Mary. 'You'll feel better after this. Fresh as a mountain spring,'

'Yes, I know, Sir Hugh. I brought it in earlier today.' Sir Hugh managed a faint smile. Mary sipped at the water. She now felt in even more of a turmoil. She was astonished that four people close to Sir Hugh had been murdered but there was no emotion. It was more like an inconvenience. Bloody hell! Mary gulped down the last bit of water. 'Thank you, Sir Hugh. I feel better now.'

'You're more than welcome, Mary. I'm glad to help.'

Mary prepared to leave the office. 'Is that all at the moment, Sir Hugh?'

'Yes, that's fine,' came the reply. Just as Mary got to the door, Sir Hugh called out, 'Another thing, Mary … have you been talking to the police?'

'Well, yes, I spoke…' Mary slightly hesitated.

Essence of Deceit by Mark Hall

Sir Hugh lowered his voice. 'Good girl, Mary. We must help the police and the detectives as best we can. You see, Mary, it's nice to be surrounded by good, decent people, people you can trust. Let me show you something.' He showed Mary a painting on the wall. 'That's a painting of Oliver Cromwell. Underneath it says, "Trust in God and keep your powder dry".' There was a small silence, then Sir Hugh turned to Mary. 'Trust, Mary. That's what it's all about. Trust is very important. Would you mind bringing me a lemon sorbet? That would be very nice.'

'Yes, of course, Sir Hugh. I'll be as quick as I can.' Mary made her way back to the kitchen. What was all that about? she pondered. Trust. Was it a veiled threat? Just then, Mary bumped into Janice, which was just as well as it stopped her mind racing into panic.

'How's it going, Mary?'

'Yeah, fine, okay.' Mary considered sharing her thoughts with Janice, but abandoned the idea and just asked how she was doing.

'The usual, busy, busy. I don't mind though, as there's less time to think about all the things going on.'

'Yeah, right,' agreed Mary.

Janice moved towards the study door and opened it then turned to her colleague and said, 'See you later.' Mary responded with a nod.

As Mary approached the kitchen door, she was conscious of voices. Just to the left, there was a fire exit door which was occasionally opened by the kitchen staff to have a quick ciggie or breather. Although the voices were low in volume, almost a whisper, they sounded quite heated. Mary was intrigued and she very quietly crept closer to the open fire exit door to try and hear more. She almost strained her ears but recognised the voices of Phil and Jed.

'What happens at the Bane-Everidge Estate stays at the Bane-Everidge Estate!' hissed Phil.

Mary sensed that they were about to move and scurried off into the kitchen to get the lemon sorbet.

*

At police HQ, the phrase was being echoed by Peter. 'What happens at the Bane-Everidge Estate is not gonna stay there much longer.' The team felt that things were on the up.

Christine and Eugene from forensics had the mobile phones out on a desk in front of them. 'Well, ladies and gentlemen, it's taken a lot of work but there's some phones here that are of particular interest ... Sir Hugh's, Phil Atkins', Diego Garcia's and Reggie Milner's,' said Christine.

Eugene continued, 'Sir Hugh's mobile is very interesting. On the day of the court case, the twenty-second of May, he paid out £300,000 to his ex-wife Cynthia Bane-Everidge. But, he normally pays out twenty grand a month. On further investigation, we found that the account numbers were different. We're still looking into this account but we've found nothing as yet. There was also £50,000 paid out to Reggie Milner with the message: *Do not mention this to ANYONE and DO NOT mention it to ME EVER.*'

The office started to hum with excited voices. Christine moved forwards. 'The phone call to Janice Brown ties in with the moment that Reggie Milner was shot. Was this coincidence or planned? There was another phone call to Alfonso Vasquez, who owns a coffee plantation in Colombia. It coincides with the time that Clive Villiers was shot.'

'Wow, we've got a bit to go on there,' Dave declared.

Essence of Deceit by Mark Hall

Fergus chimed in, 'What do you know? A coffee plantation in Colombia. Ha ha! Pull the other one, it's got bells on.'

'As for Reggie Milner, it could have been what the butler might have seen,' Heather wondered. Dave nodded in agreement.

Christine continued, 'With regards to the chauffeur, Diego Garcia, everything appears above board, including texts and phone calls to family. Also his contact with Alfonso Vasquez looks okay but needs a bit more studying.'

Eugene picked up the phone that belonged to Phil Atkins. 'Now this gentlemen, Mr Atkins … we found threatening texts to the deceased chef, Ben Charles, and threats to Gary Hinchcliffe. Wasn't he the first chauffeur?' he asked Dave.

'He was,' Dave replied quietly.

'He also threatened Jed Mullins and then gave a rambling apology about brotherly love. This Atkins is quite a charmer. Janice Brown also received a terse text. There's more.' Eugene looked at the phone. 'Here we are. He threatened the gardener, Archie Sangster, with: *You effing two-bit gardener. You don't know who you're messing with. Don't upset me, otherwise you'll end up with a bigger lump on your head than you have on your back, you ugly git.*

Obviously, there's plenty on this phone to have a look at and I think his picture gallery will be interesting too, so good luck team.'

Peter stepped forwards. 'Thank you both. That's been a great help. Thank the rest of your guys too.'

Christine commented on their progress. 'We're still looking into the other mobile phones and of course the emails. And, as you know, nothing has been left at the scene of the crimes.'

'Yeah,' replied Peter, 'but we've got a good bit to go on with the mobiles at the moment. Thanks again.' Christine and Eugene made their way out of the office.

As soon as the office door was shut, the CID office broke into noise and discussion. Claire raised a point with Fergus. 'Can you remember when we were at the house and Phil Atkins brought in Archie Sangster. The gardener looked worse for wear. I reckon that Atkins roughed him up then.'

'I think you're right,' answered Fergus. 'He's a nasty little piece. I would love to give him the Glasgow kiss.'

Heather pulled an inquisitive face. 'What's that?'

'A head butt!'

Claire answered, 'Yeah, a bit of Glaswegian hospitality.'

'Just what Atkins needs,' added Fergus.

The CID team started to study the mobile phones. Peter looked at Sir Hugh's phone, while Heather studied Phil Atkins' mobile.

'Any pictures of the party?' enquired Peter.

'Nah, haven't seen any yet.'

The rest of the team were looking at Diego Garcia's phone and Reggie Milner's phone. The atmosphere in the office was one of quiet concentration. Dave joined Heather and looked over her shoulder. Peter was just about to say something.

'Hey, look at this,' exclaimed Heather. 'Tenton Gun Club, runner up, 2013.' The whole team got interested and looked up. She continued to scroll through the pictures. 'Oh my God! Can you believe this?' she said with a mixture of bemusement and amusement. The team crowded round.

Heather kept the running commentary going. 'Look at this picture. This is Atkins in his Calvin Klein underpants posing with a rifle with a fat cigar in his mouth and a red baseball cap with the words "hot shot" emblazoned on it.'

'What do you make of that?' Dave enquired.

Spyros turned to Peter. 'Is he our man, sir?'

'It would be a stroke of luck if he was. But did he have the windows of opportunity? Doubtful.' Peter blew out through his lips and put a hand through his hair.

'He certainly knows the gaff. He could just quickly disappear from the kitchen. Boom! Then back to work again,' explained Spyros. The team aired their views. It was a mixture of possibles and unlikelys.

Peter decided to push the investigation forward. He stood up from his chair. 'Carry on, guys. I'll be one moment.' He marched to his private office and phoned Sergeant Peters. The Sergeant answered the phone immediately. 'How's it going down there?' enquired Peter.

'You know, so-so. We're still parading the grounds.'

'Sergeant, I want you to bring in the following people for questioning – Phil Atkins Diego Garcia, Mary Edmunds and Sir Hugh.'

'Got that, sir. Will do.'

Peter went back into the main office and updated the team on the latest news.

Essence of Deceit by Mark Hall

*

At the Bane-Everidge Estate, Mary went back to Sir Hugh's office to collect any crockery or cutlery that had been finished with. As she entered the office, Sir Hugh was sitting at his desk with a duster, going over the picture of Oliver Cromwell. Mary collected the plates, dishes, knives and forks. Sir Hugh didn't look up but managed to grunt a thanks. Mary didn't ask whether Sir Hugh required anything else and just slid out of the room.

In the kitchen, Phil had lost the plot. The 'hot shot' was very hot headed and he'd just had a big verbal altercation with Jed. As for Mary, he thought to himself, he was going to teach her a lesson. He was gonna scare the living daylights out of her which would make her think twice about gobbing off to the police. Phil decided to slip out of the kitchen. 'I'll be two minutes, Carl.' Carl replied, 'Okay', but Phil hardly noticed.

He ran to the living quarters. He went inside and along a small corridor. He got his door key out and went into his room. There was nothing flash here. The room was small and basic. All the living quarters were basically the same with a shower bathroom, small bedroom, kitchen and lounge area.

Essence of Deceit by Mark Hall

Phil opened a long narrow cupboard, which was a place for brooms, mops and an ironing board. He put a fishing rod bag to one side and pulled out a leather bag which resembled a fishing case but didn't contain any fishing rods. He unzipped it and pulled out a rifle. 'I'd better unload it,' he said to himself. 'I don't want to hurt anyone but if she keeps on snitching…' He hurried himself, grabbed a large bath towel and covered the gun then closed the cupboard door discreetly and swiftly left the living quarters.

Phil made his way around the back of the kitchen to the bin area. He lay down flat in position, armed and ready to scare the life out of Mary. He allowed himself a slight giggle. Minutes passed. 'Come on, Edmunds. I haven't got all day. You've surely got to come up here, back to the kitchen, or to the launderette.'

Another minute or so passed by. The hot headed Phil was cooling down. He realised that he'd taken the prank too far. It was a really stupid mistake. He decided to abandon the idea then he noticed a police officer down by the front of the house. He couldn't move yet. He didn't want to be seen. As soon as the officer walked back the other way, he would clear off.

But Phil had been seen. He was being watched very intently. The eyes lasered onto him, watching his every move. Precise calculations were being processed. This certainly hadn't been on the agenda. This irritant had got to go. The killer breathed out long and slow. This was tricky, very tricky. The killer decided that it was now time for something different.

The movement was swift and silent. An arm locked around the neck. A hard finger to a nerve point. Phil Atkins was temporarily knocked out. Atkin's gun was unlocked. The killer was surprised that the clown hadn't even loaded it. The killer put a bullet into the rifle. The bullet fitted.

The assassin laid Atkins in the correct sniper's position, holding the rifle. He would soon wake. The police had to be alerted and Atkins caught red-handed. Swiftly and stealthily, the assassin moved towards the kitchen. The window of opportunity was now the size of a keyhole and rapidly disappearing. If anyone came out of the kitchen door... Also, police officers could be seen moving around. Not far from the kitchen door there was a fire alarm. The assassin gave it a whack. Rrrriinnnnngg! The alarm was loud, clear and constant. The killer sprinted to the back of the kitchen, into the woods and was gone.

Police arrived from all areas. It was almost as though the assassin had summoned up the gods, because an armed officer, Graham Miles, arrived behind Atkins and announced the immortal words, 'POLICE! HANDS OFF THE WEAPON AND HANDS BEHIND YOUR BACK!'

Phil began to stir. He was still groggy, unbeknown to Graham, who barked the commands again as Phil was moving too slow for his liking. 'HEY!'

Phil obliged and Graham moved in, kicking the gun away and skilfully and deftly cable-tying Phil's wrists. He then told Phil the police procedure clearly and precisely. 'I am arresting you on suspicion of using a firearm with intent to endanger life or cause harm. You do not have to say anything. But, it may harm your defence if you do not mention when questioned something which you later rely on in court. Anything you do say may be given in evidence.' Phil was then pulled up onto his feet.

More officers arrived at the scene. Jed came out of the kitchen and stopped the fire alarm. Graham was marching Phil along, holding him tightly under control with his left hand. He carried Phil's rifle in his right hand. They walked along the side of the kitchen.

Jed's jaw dropped open and, for once, he was lost for words. Carl stumbled out of the kitchen door. 'What the hell! Phil, Phil, what's going on?'

Phil tried to turn, but he couldn't manage it because he was being held too tightly by Graham. He managed to shout out, 'I'm innocent. I'm innocent. This was only a joke!'

Graham very quickly came to the understanding that this gentleman was going to be difficult and awkward. He gave Phil a gentle reminder and virtually growled in his ear, 'It will be in your best interests if you fully cooperate with the police.'

The police and the staff of the house were congregating. Sergeant Peters took control.

'Please can you two police officers accompany firearms officer Graham Miles and the suspect back to HQ.'

'Okay, Sarg, will do.' The four of them walked off down to the front of the house, across the manicured lawns to the parked vehicles.

Essence of Deceit by Mark Hall

The Bane-Everidge staff watched another episode unfold with utter bewilderment and disbelief. All of the staff were there, discussing the events. Archie Sangster asked the kitchen boys, 'Is that our man? Is that the gunman? Have they caught him?'

'God knows, Archie. I'm absolutely baffled. I don't know what's going on,' replied Carl.

Jed added his opinion. 'I can't see Phil being a killer. I really can't. I know he's an absolute pain in the rear at times with the stupid pranks he gets up to, but being a killer … Nah! I didn't even know he had a rifle.'

Archie then shared a conversation he'd had with Phil. 'He likes a bit of fishing and occasionally he shoots rabbits. He also told me he belonged to a gun club. He reckons he's at a high standard.'

Jed said nothing and just wondered. He knew that Phil was a hot head because he'd had a few run-ins with him, but surely Phil wouldn't go to the level of being a killer. Jed dismissed the thought.

Carl joined in, 'Don't believe everything Phil says. He's a bit of a bullshitter.'

Sir Hugh eventually turned up. 'What's going on? What's happened now? I heard the fire alarm. There's not a fire in the kitchen is there?'

Janice was standing next to Gina and Mary. 'Well, erm...' Janice paused and stumbled. 'You're not going to believe this but...'

Sir Hugh was losing patience. 'Come on, Janice, get on with it.'

'Well, Phil Atkins was caught in possession of a rifle and he's been arrested. So there you are, Sir Hugh.' Janice felt irritated by Sir Hugh and showed her displeasure by pulling a discreet face at Gina and Mary.

Sir Hugh shook his head and mumbled, 'I don't believe this.'

Sergeant Peters, after directing the uniform boys, approached the staff. He looked around at the staff and then said to Sir Hugh, 'Where is your chauffeur, Diego Garcia?'

Sir Hugh craned his neck around and stood on tiptoes. 'Ah, there he is.' He pointed to the left. 'He's over there, Sergeant, having a cigarette.'

Sergeant Peters indicated to an officer to go and get Diego, who was standing about twenty yards away. 'Okay, Sir Hugh, this is what's happening. I would like you, Diego Garcia and Mary Edmunds to come to the station with us.'

'I'm sorry, Sergeant. I'm not going to talk to anyone without a lawyer,' said Sir Hugh. 'I told your CID colleagues this.'

'Okay, Sir Hugh, we'll take Diego Garcia and Mary Edmunds. You can sort out your lawyer and get a lift to the station with DI Thompson and the rest of the team because they'll be here in about forty-five minutes. That should give you enough time to sort things out.'

Sir Hugh protested, 'That's ridiculous. There's no time at all.'

'What? A man of your calibre and standing, Sir Hugh. I thought you would just click your fingers…'

Sir Hugh had taken a large dislike to Sergeant Peters. He was about to give him a verbal what for, but decided to bite his tongue.

*

Back at HQ, a call had come in from Sergeant Peters and the CID team had been fully updated on the big bombshell that Phil Atkins had been arrested with a rifle.

'Told you he was dodgy,' Claire quipped.

'Is he the assassin?' enquired Spyros.

'He's been caught red-handed with a rifle. It's looking probable. I wonder who he was gunning for this time? Uniform boys are bringing him in. He can go in a cell and stew for a bit while we question the others,' said Peter. He continued talking, outlining what was happening. 'They're also bringing in Diego Garcia and Mary Edmunds. Sir Hugh is jumping up and down because he wants a lawyer. By the time we get over there, he should have a lawyer sorted and I'll bring him in with Fergus. Dave, can you and the team question Diego Garcia and Mary Edmunds. When they get here, use interview rooms one and three, thanks. Okay, team, onwards and upwards. Catch you later.'

Peter and Fergus walked briskly away from the headquarters. They both climbed into the four-by-four, with Peter driving, and headed off once more to the Bane-Everidge Estate.

Not long after Fergus and Peter had left, Phil Atkins arrived at the police station. Dave took the walk through the building to 'observe' the arrival of Atkins. The formalities and procedures took place at the desk. The suspect was taken to a cell. Not much was said or discussed, but Dave remarked, 'Keep an eye on him. He's a crafty one.'

'Will do, sir,' came the reply from the officer.

Dave marched back to the office. 'Okay, team, listen up. Phil Atkins is here. He's in a cell and we'll deal with him later. Heather and I will question Diego Garcia in an interview. Spyros and Claire, can you question Mary Edmunds in room three.' Dave looked at his watch. 'They should be here very shortly.'

*

At the Bane-Everidge Estate, Peter and Fergus arrived and parked up. As the pair climbed out of the vehicle, they were greeted by two armed officers. The four of them discussed the arrest of Phil Atkins, then they parted ways and the two armed officers went back to their task.

Peter and Fergus went up the steps to the main front door. Janice opened the door before Peter pressed the bell.

'Hi,' Janice greeted.

'Hello, Janice,' replied Peter. Fergus just nodded. 'Where is Sir Hugh? Is he in his office? he enquired.

'Yes, I think he is. Shall I go and get him or notify him you're here?' Janice answered. 'No thank you, Janice. Leave it to us, thank you.' With that, the two detectives marched towards the office. The pair stood at the office door and Peter administered a polite knock. Nothing happened. He knocked on the door louder, waited a couple of seconds then opened the door. 'Hello? Hello, Sir Hugh? It's DI Thompson and DC Ferguson here.'

There was no sign of Sir Hugh. Fergus loved having a nose around, which irritated his boss, he'd often been told. But he didn't care one bit. The Glaswegian hovered around Sir Hugh's desk like a wasp around a marmalade jar. 'Aye, will you get a load of this!' Face up on the desk was a picture of Oliver Cromwell.

Fergus carried on and read aloud, '"...trust in God and keep your powder dry". What's all that about?'

Peter moved over to join Fergus for a better look. He moved the picture. Scribbled on a notepad was the word 'TRUST' in block capital letters. The word was almost written again but the pencil had broken. Peter and Fergus looked at each other. They said nothing but both detectives realised that someone or something had hit a nerve of Sir Hugh.

After five to ten minutes, Peter decided it was time to leave the office and actually find Sir Hugh. 'Come on, Fergus. Let's go and find the main man.'

The pair left the office and headed towards the dining room. Peter opened the door and the pair walked through. 'Hello, Sir Hugh. Are you ready to accompany us to the station?'

'Well, just about. I managed to get a lawyer. He'll meet us down there.'

Sir Hugh and the two detectives walked down the hallway to the reception area. As they reached the front door, Janice was there.

'Janice, you've got the reins now. I'm sure everything will be fine and I won't be long. Good luck,' said Sir Hugh.

Janice managed a small smile. 'Bye, Sir Hugh.' She opened the door. The three of them left the building, climbed into the four-by-four and were gone. Janice watched the vehicle go down the driveway. She closed the door, locked it, then leaned back on it and let out a massive sigh.

*

At the police headquarters, in the interview rooms, the CID team were questioning Diego Garcia and Mary Edmunds. In room one, Diego sat opposite Dave and Heather. On the table to one side, various pieces of equipment were laid out – a recording machine, writing pads, pencils and Diego's mobile phone. Heather went through the usual procedure and protocol.

Dave wasted no time. 'Now, Mr Garcia. Do you know a gentleman by the name of Alfonso Vasquez?'

'Well, yes, he's an old friend.'

'How long have you known him?' pursued Dave.

'I suppose ten to twelve years,' Garcia replied.

'How did you meet Mr Vasquez?'

'He used to sponsor the football team my son played in.'

Dave carried on, 'Go on, Mr Garcia. Tell us more.'

'What? He sponsored my son's football team.'

Heather joined in. 'Mr Garcia, we're trying to establish your connection with Alfonso Vasquez.'

The chauffeur shrugged his shoulders and pulled a face. 'I've just told you.' Dave and Heather exchanged glances. They knew that Diego wasn't playing ball.

Dave started to slowly turn up the heat. 'You've known Mr Vasquez for twelve years. We've established that he sponsored your son's football team. We also know that he owns a big coffee plantation. It's a large business and he's a considerably wealthy gentleman. Your friend knows lots of influential people, people in high places, and, of course, very close to Sir Hugh.' The chauffeur listened intently.

Heather took up the questioning. 'Why did you come here to work for Sir Hugh?'

'I wanted more money. My son is going through college back home and my daughter struggles with two young daughters of her own. Her husband just upped and left one day. She never heard a thing from him. My wife and I do what we can but it's tough.'

'You have our sympathy, Mr Garcia, but please do carry on,' said Dave, taking over the questioning from Heather.

'Mr Vasquez knew about the vacancy for a chauffeur so he gave me a call and put me in touch with Sir Hugh. I thought, why not? I speak good English. I was a taxi driver back home. This is more money. Although I miss my family, I thought it would be a good opportunity to get some money behind us. That's the truth. I've done nothing wrong. I don't even know why I'm being questioned.'

Dave took a second. 'Well, just to remind you, there's been four shootings. That's just for starters. The chauffeur that you replaced disappeared off the map with a so-called retirement. So, your friend Alfonso put you in touch with Sir Hugh?' Diego nodded his head. 'Here's the thing, Mr Garcia. It's all around the time of the court case.'

With that, Diego stood up. 'I've done nothing wrong. Nothing. I'm a good man. I'm here for my family.'

'Please sit down, Mr Garcia. Take a breath. We just have a couple more questions.' Heather's soft tone cooled the situation. Reluctantly and slowly, Diego sat back down.

Dave and Heather examined the mobile data sheet from forensics. Heather also looked over the mobile phone.

Dave mentioned some very short text messages. 'There's one here from Sam Garcia: *Are you okay. Dad?* That's obviously your son then, Mr Garcia?'

'Yes, Sam is my son.'

The two detectives kept looking.

'There's a text here from Alfonso Vasquez: *Are you okay?* And you reply with a thumbs up. Very short and sweet. There's another three short sweet texts from Mr Vasquez and they're all exactly the same. But what's really interesting, Mr Garcia, is the dates. The first text is the twenty-second of May, which was the end of the court case when Roland Van Mendes was shot dead. The second text is the twenty-fourth of May when Ben Charles was shot dead. The third text is the twenty-seventh of May when Reggie Milner was shot dead and, finally, the fourth text is on the date when Clive Villiers was shot dead.' Both detectives stared at Diego and there was silence.

Dave let Diego ponder his thoughts then asked, 'What have you got to say about that, Mr Garcia?'

Diego looked nonplussed and shrugged his shoulders. 'Mr Vasquez checked to see if I was okay.'

Dave stood up and leaned forwards. 'The dates, Mr Garcia, the dates!'

'I've told you. I've done nothing wrong. Mr Vasquez checked to see if I was okay because of the shootings. He cares for me.'

Dave then asked, 'How did your Colombian friend know about the shootings?' 'Probably Sir Hugh. They're good friends. You know this.'

Dave had had enough and went in strong. 'I reckon that the thumbs up that you sent in the texts meant "job done". Eliminated. Rubbed out. Cleaned up.'

Diego stood up and his chair fell backwards to the floor. He hollered at the two detectives, 'You are pigs and this is total and utter rubbish. You two are stupid pigs.'

'I would advise you, Mr Garcia, to ease it down a bit. It would be in your best interests,' Dave interjected.

'How could it be me? I was driving the limousine when Van Mendes got shot.'

'What about the other three?' asked Heather.

Diego's emotions had eased down. He was still standing and leaned on the back of the chair. He let out a wry smile. 'This really has been a waste of time. You've arrested the wrong man. You've got the gunman in a cell. It's Phil Atkins.'

'We're covering all angles, Mr Garcia. We're looking at the bigger picture. All the details. It's all been a bit smoke and mirrors.' Dave's eyes bored into the chauffeur with great intensity, using his years of experience as a detective. He'd seen the lot – barefaced liars, slippery deceivers, poker-faced criminals. His eyes kept scanning, searching for any indication at all of what Diego was hiding. He noticed a small quiver at the top of Diego's left cheek. 'Mr Garcia,

DC Barnes and I are just going to take a moment outside. Please excuse us.'

Heather turned off the recording machine. Uniformed police came in and stood by the door. The pair of CIDs exited the room, shutting the door.

'He's hiding something, I'm sure of it,' declared Dave.

'Well, he didn't shoot Van Mendes, but there's, as you say, the other three. But we've caught Phil Atkins red-handed.' Heather continued, 'I agree with you that Diego Garcia is hiding something. As for pulling the trigger...' She let out a long sigh. 'Mm ... but yes, he DOES know something.'

'Right, this is what's going to happen,' decided Dave. 'We'll tell that Columbian that he has to stay in the cells for tonight. We've got Phil Atkins, so maybe, just maybe, he's the one and we have to look no further. Let's do this.'

Dave and Heather opened the door and marched in. 'Mr Garcia, that's all the questioning for now. You'll be here for tonight. We'll talk again tomorrow.'

Surprisingly, Diego said nothing. Dave indicated to the police officers to take Diego Garcia to the cells.

Essence of Deceit by Mark Hall

*

In interview room three, Spyros and Clare were interviewing Mary Edmunds. The usual police procedures and protocol were followed. Claire pressed the recording machine and kicked off the questioning. 'Mary, we just want to go over a few things.'

'I don't know why you're questioning me. It's Phil Atkins you need to speak to. He's the criminal. Go and speak to him.'

'Don't worry about him. He's not going anywhere. He won't run off,' Spyros added.   Clare started again. 'Mary, tell us what you know about Phil Atkins.'

'You caught him with a gun. Well, not you personally, but the other police officers. He was caught lying down near the bin area and kitchen.' Mary became anxious and panicky.

'You okay?' asked Spyros.

'Yeah, I'm okay.' Mary struggled on. 'I think that Phil was waiting for me with his gun. I know he doesn't like me.'

'What makes you say that?' Claire asked.

'I went into the kitchen to collect Sir Hugh's lunch and Phil looked at me with this horrendous stare.' Perhaps he's been taught by my colleague, Clare the glare, Spyros thought.

Essence of Deceit by Mark Hall

'He looked so evil, so scary.' Mary paused and again looked panicky. 'He looked like he wanted to kill me.'

'Why would he want to do that, Mary?' Clare asked.

'I ... I don't know. Well, he did go funny after I spoke to you at the house. He might know that I told you that I saw him at the party. You didn't tell him, did you?'

'No, of course not, Mary.' Claire continued, 'Are you quite sure you saw Phil Atkins at the party?'

'I saw him briefly. It was quite late. He was just flitting about, you know.'

Spyros then asked, 'Did he actually stop and talk to anybody?'

Mary put her hand to her chin and thought carefully. 'Yes, he did spend a little bit of time with Diego Garcia.'

'Okay,' Claire responded and added that to her notes.

Spyros carried on with the questioning. 'Is there anybody else that Phil Atkins dislikes, Mary?'

'He does have these mood swings. He can be quite nasty. He doesn't mind playing a joke or a prank, but he doesn't like jokes being made about him. Come to think of it, when I went back to the kitchen to get Sir Hugh a sorbet, I heard him secretly arguing with Jed Mullins. It sounded quite heated and they were both trying hard to keep the volume down. They were outside, at the back of the kitchen.'

'Any idea what that was about?' Claire asked

'I'm not too sure. I tried to listen discreetly, but I was scared of getting caught. But I did manage to hear Phil say something like "what happens in this estate stays in this estate"'.

'It sounds like he's up to no good,' Spyros added.

It went quiet in the interview room. Mary sat there thinking and looking uncomfortable. Both detectives observed this. Spyros glanced at Claire to take the initiative. Clare waited for a moment then she leaned towards Mary. 'There's something else bothering you, isn't there?'

'Er ... no,' replied Mary. She fidgeted and looked awkward.

The detective moved closer, not in an intimidating way, but just closing the space. She adopted a gentle manner. 'Are you sure there's nothing you're not telling us?'

Mary couldn't contain herself any longer and blurted out, 'It's Sir Hugh...' Spyros and Claire sat upright in their chairs.

'Go on, Mary,' Claire prompted.

'He's been really odd as well with me since I spoke to you people.'

'How do you mean?' Claire added.

'When I took lunch to his office, he was really weird. He asked me whether I'd spoken to you people, which he knows anyway. He then said he was very pleased and he was desperate to catch the killer. Then he went very serious. He was a bit scary. I didn't like it.' 'Oh really! Can you explain a bit more?' asked Spyros.

'He pointed to a picture on the wall of some famous history person, Oliver Cramwell.' 'Oliver Cromwell,' Claire corrected.

'Yes, that's him. There was something written on the picture, something to do with trust and Sir Hugh made a big thing about it.' Mary became agitated, then she started to panic. 'Not long after I saw Sir Hugh, Phil was arrested with a rifle. You don't think they're in this together? They don't trust me. Sir Hugh must have told Phil to shoot me. That's it! They're in this together if Sir Hugh doesn't trust anyone. Oh my God!' Mary was getting in a right state. Both detectives stood up, trying to calm her down. 'It's your fault. You must have told them I saw Phil Atkins at the party.'

Clare got hold of Mary's arms. 'Come on, Mary, come on. Deep breaths. Nothing is going to happen to you. You're perfectly safe. Only the police know about your statements. No one else.'

Spyros passed Mary a glass of water. She took a sip. 'Do you think they're in this together ... Phil and Sir Hugh?' she asked.

Clare was relieved that Mary had come back to some sort of normality and answered her question. 'It's like this. We're gathering lots of information, bit by bit. It's like a jigsaw. Very soon we'll have the whole picture.'

The three of them stood up together. The detectives finished the interview, and went through the usual procedures. Time was getting on. Mary left the building and ordered a taxi back to the Bane-Everidge Estate, free from questioning, for the time being.

*

Peter drove into the car park of the police station and CID headquarters, accompanied by Fergus and Sir Hugh. He parked up and the trio climbed out. They entered the building through the double doors, and walked along the corridor to interview room two.

Sir Hugh sat down opposite Peter and Fergus. The chair next to Sir Hugh was empty. Fergus busied himself with police paraphernalia and getting ready for the interview. 'My lawyer isn't here so I'm not talking,' Sir Hugh declared.

Peter's jaw tightened. Here we go, he thought. 'Do you have your lawyer's phone number, Sir Hugh?'

'Well, yes, it's in my phone, which you have.'

Peter picked up Sir Hugh's phone. 'What's his name, Sir Hugh?'

'Steven Benson.'

Peter fiddled with the phone and managed to get through. 'Hello, is that Steven Benson? This is DI Peter Thompson. I understand that you're representing Sir Hugh Bane-Everidge.' He paused to listen. 'We're all here now. Ready to go.' He looked at Fergus with an expression of annoyance and disbelief then held the phone to his chest and looked at Sir Hugh. 'Your lawyer, Mr Benson, can't make it this evening because of a family emergency.'

Sir Hugh raised his eyebrows and tutted loudly. 'This is ridiculous. How unprofessional! Roland was never like this. A family emergency, you say? Well, I hope everyone is alright. When can he come in then?'

Peter put the phone to his ear. 'Yes, fine. We'll do that. Thank you. Tomorrow, eight-thirty am sharp.'

Sir Hugh stood up. 'Now what?'

Peter explained the procedure to Sir Hugh that he would spend the night in the cells. Peter and Fergus were surprised by his reaction. The detectives had expected some sort of resistance or a mini drama, but Sir Hugh was very compliant and just uttered the word, 'Fine.'

The three of them exited the room and started to walk down the corridor towards the cells. They were joined by two uniformed officers. One of them felt the urge to guide Sir Hugh by gently putting his arm around Sir Hugh's back.

'Get your hand off me. Touch me again and I'll file a complaint,' Sir Hugh said.

They reached the cell. Locks and keys rattled and the door swung open. Sir Hugh walked in and sat himself on the bed.

'Would you like a bite to eat, sir? A sandwich and a cup of tea?'

'What have you got?' asked Sir Hugh.

'Cheese and pickle, ham and tomato, tuna mayo and cucumber.'

'I'll have cheese and pickle and a tea. Have you got Earl Grey?'

'I don't think so, sir. I'm sure we haven't got that one. How about Tetley in a mug, is that okay for you?' The hint of sarcasm was missed by Sir Hugh but Fergus winked at the officer. Peter quickly briefed the officers about Sir Hugh and the uniform boys took it from there.

Peter and Fergus headed back to the office for a quick update with the rest of the team. There was the full team in the office. Fergus sat down and Peter took his usual place standing at the front. 'Okay, we'll start with Dave and Heather. How did it go?'

'Yes, as you know, we interviewed the chauffeur, Diego Garcia. Obviously, it's all recorded but we'll give you the bones of it.' Dave nodded towards Heather to proceed.

'Diego Garcia told us that he is over here quite innocently to earn more money to support his family. It appears that Sir Hugh contacted Alfonso Vasquez, who then in turn contacted Diego

Garcia. As you will hear in the recording, the intriguing thing is the dates and the short text messages. When we pushed him in the interview, he became angry and emotional.'

Dave joined in, 'Heather and I both agree that he knows more than he's letting on.'

Peter put his hand to his chin and, after slight pause, said, 'Okay, thank you both. We'll go through the recording tomorrow. It's good that he's under lock and key. Clare and Spyros, what about Mary Edmunds?'

Claire proceeded to give an outline of the interview. 'We can all certainly agree on one thing, that Phil Atkins is a nasty piece of work. Mary Edmunds thought or suggested that Atkins was the killer.'

Peter chipped in, 'It's a tricky one that. Obviously, we'll grill him tomorrow. I think it would have been too difficult for him to shoot four people and not get caught. I do wonder about the chef, though.'

Dave joined the discussion. 'I don't buy it with Atkins. I still think it's a slick professional.'

Essence of Deceit by Mark Hall

The office hummed with conversation regarding the latest interviews. Claire then mentioned Sir Hugh and the picture of trust. Peter and Fergus also shared their views about that subject. Clare brought up the fact that Mary Edmunds believed that Sir Hugh and Phil Atkins were in the whole scenario together. The team's opinions were mixed.

After a while, Peter clapped his hands. The talking stopped and heads turned towards the boss. 'Okay, team, thanks for all your hard work. Tomorrow, we'll grill, and I mean grill, Phil Atkins and Sir Hugh. We'll pack up now. Have a restful evening. Have three Weetabix in the morning and be here at eight o'clock sharp.'

The CID team left the building and went their separate ways. There was another life other than detective work. No one hung about in the car park. They were all off and gone.

*

Fergus bowled in at home, into the kitchen and playfully grabbed his wife, Carol. 'Have you not got the dinner on yet?' was his opening line.

'Youse got some cheek. Coming in here barking orders,' replied Carol. They'd been childhood sweethearts, Carol and Bill, both brought up in a tough part of Glasgow. Quite a passionate and explosive mix, but solid as a rock.

Spyros and his wife Anna had been round for a meal at the Ferguson's. Spyros had jokingly said, 'My wife and I need subtitles to understand you two.' But a great night had been had. Fergus was overgenerous with the 'fire water' and Spyros had vowed to never ever touch whisky again.

Carol was busying herself in the kitchen. Spaghetti bolognese was on the menu. The pair exchanged small talk, with Carol telling Fergus that she was in a bit late. She'd beaten her mate Holly at squash, which was something considering she'd lost about half a dozen games on the trot. After a while, Carol told Fergus to get out of the way and take a shower. Fergus went off to a big splash in the shower and a wee splash of Glenfiddich.

Generally, across the team of detectives, it was shower or bath, evening meal and chill out. Clare was curled up on the settee with Bonzo and Fred, her two beloved cats, watching *The Terminator* for the umpteenth time. Dave was virtually horizontal on the settee, flicking through the channels on the TV remote, while his wife was stuck on a crossword puzzle. Downtime was fairly relaxed and uneventful, although Heather was giving her husband, Niles, a hard time playing poker.

There were two members of the team not exactly having a hard time, but they certainly weren't relaxed.

*

Spyros decided to do a small weight training session in the spare room upstairs. He couldn't find his tracksuit bottoms and called to his wife Anna who was downstairs, 'Anna, darling, have you seen my grey tracksuit bottoms?'

Anna shouted the reply, 'Try the washing basket.'

Spyros did just that and rummaged through. He found the tracksuit bottoms. They would do for tonight, he thought. He shoved them on, then he got a jolt. He picked up the pair of dark green trousers, the pair he'd worn at the Bane-Everidge Estate. Kay's earrings. His mind started racing. Hell, if Anna found them how was he going to explain that one? What if there was only one? Was the earring found at the swimming pool really Kay's? Although, thank God, there was no DNA.

Spyros started to sweat. He reached deep into the pocket. Aaahhh, gotcha, he thought, and pulled out the stud earring. Curious, he put his hand back in. He could feel something tight in the corner. With a bit more fiddling, he pulled out the second earring. He felt absolutely jubilant. He went back to the spare room, clutching the earrings tight in his hand. He walked over to the dumbbell weights, to a small chest of drawers. He pulled open the top drawer and managed to find a small envelope. He put both earrings inside and sealed it down. He then went to his car and put them in the side door compartment. He thought that was probably the safest and most discreet place to put them.

Spyros went back in the house, went upstairs and carried on rummaging through the chest of drawers. There was all sorts in there – batteries, felt pens, assorted loose change and foreign coins, kickboxing medals, third and fourth place. They hadn't been good enough to show off. The first place trophy was downstairs in the living room.

He found what he was looking for, an old mobile phone which was a very good spare. He kept it charged up regularly. He sat on the weights bench and scrolled through the phone, looking at the contacts. He came to the letter K and paused. Should he ring or not?

he thought. Spyros pressed the dial button. He could hear the dialling tone and his heartbeat went up. She was like a drug.

Moments later, Kay answered the phone. 'Hello, who's this?'

'It's me, Spyros,' he said in a hushed voice.

'Wait a minute,' came the terse reply.

Spyros sensed that Kay was moving to another room to be more discreet. He got off the weights bench to gently close the door.

'What are you doing ringing me? I thought we'd agreed not to ring each other. You know what my husband's like. If he gets wind of this…'

'Yes, I know, Kay. I'm sorry. I found both of your ear studs. You left them at the health centre, do you remember?'

'Yeah, yeah, course I did, thanks. Brill.'

Spyros continued, 'I'll tell you what I'll do. I'll leave them at reception at the health club in the next day or two.'

'Er, yeah, fine, yeah, thanks.' Kay sounded edgy. 'I appreciate that. I'll pick them up when I can. I've got another pair, very similar, but I lost one of those recently. I can't think where. I've got to go now. Peter's coming.' The phone cut off abruptly.

Spyros sat at the weights bench, picked up the dumbbells, and commenced to do front presses. He did repetitions then put the weights down. A little niggle dug into his mind. Kay had lost an earring. He swore under his breath then dismissed it. He picked up the weights to do another seven.

*

At the Thompson household, Peter was struggling to switch off. Kay had remarked, a number of times, that her husband was always on duty. A couple of factors hadn't helped. The obvious early retirement of Kay from the police force and also the quiet whisperings about Spyros. Peter had tried in the past to talk to Kay about those two subjects. She flatly and vehemently denied any wrongdoing and considered the matters closed. Finito!

Peter was now even more edgy. His wife had taken a phone call but it was her manner and her body language and the way she'd crept off to the dining room that had aroused his suspicion. Was it twenty-four seven professionalism, or paranoia, or even a bit of both? It was hard to say.

Kay walked back into the lounge then announced she was off for a shower. Peter replied he was going to have another glass of wine and watch a bit more TV.

He waited a couple of seconds until his wife was up the stairs then went into the kitchen. The wine bottle was still out. He poured just over half a glass. Left of the bottle was Kay's mobile phone. A little bit of brief manipulation and Peter was looking through recent calls. Nothing. His wife must have erased them. He looked at recent text messages. Nothing untoward there.

Peter put the phone back, picked up his wine went back to the lounge. *Newsnight* came on the TV and he got comfy, Yeah, he'd have a bit of this, he thought. But within minutes, his attention went back to his wife's phone call. He wondered who it had been. He'd better not ask. She would go nuclear. There was nothing unusual in her clearing the phone, apart from a couple of texts. She was always super tidy, super organised. Nothing out of place. When she'd worked in the force, she'd quite often said, 'Details and precision. If it's not needed, bin it or delete it.'

When she'd worked in the office with CID for a brief time, before she moved on to the gun squad and undercover, she'd upset

Fergus about him being untidy, which was nothing. But it had got out of hand. She'd said icily to the Glaswegian, 'A good cleaner wouldn't go amiss in here. They could eradicate the unwanted trash.'

Kay had walked off and Fergus had blown his top and had to be calmed down by Clare and Heather. But he'd still managed to shout, 'Get your mop and bucket then.'

Peter smirked to himself then muttered, 'I don't know.' But very slowly he had this awful feeling. The way his wife was talking, she'd meant cleaner all right. She'd meant professional hitman. His mind started racing. The scratches on the side of her face. Was she in the bushes at the Bane-Everidge Estate? The earring? No, it couldn't be. There'd been no DNA. Precision, details. He held his breath No, it couldn't be true. He was just making pieces fit to suit.

He exhaled loudly, stood up and turned the TV off. Then he went to the kitchen to rinse his glass. Well, they had Atkins caught red-handed. With that, Peter finally relaxed then went to bed.

*

At police HQ, at eight am, the CID team were all assembled, alert and ready for the day ahead.

Peter opened up proceedings. 'Morning all.'

'Morning, sir,' the team responded in unison.

'Wow, all synchronised together there. We should form a choir.' The team laughed. Peter stood in front of the incident board. 'So, we have three suspects. Phil Atkins, because of the firearm, and Sir Hugh, because of suspicious payments out of his bank account.' Spyros looked puzzled. 'I'll jog your memories. Forensics traced it.'

'Oh, yeah, got it,' replied Spyros.

'And Diego Garcia. Phil Atkins and Sir Hugh are obvious. Diego Garcia is a tricky dicky, plus he has links to Alfonso Vasquez, the Colombian 'coffee dealer'. Is Diego Garcia a person of interest or a suspect? Okay, myself and Fergus will be in interview room two with Sir Hugh. Dave and Heather will be in room four with Phil Atkins. And in room one will be Spyros and Clare to see if they can unravel anything more from Diego Garcia. Okay, good luck everybody.'

The noise of chairs being pushed back or dragged filled the room. The team of detectives were out of the door and ready to get down to business.

*

In interview room two, Peter and Fergus stood next to two empty chairs. Moments later, two police officers escorted Sir Hugh and his lawyer, Steven Benson, into the room. They automatically sat in the two seats across the table from the detectives. Steven opened his briefcase, took out a small folder and a pen. Peter went through the usual routine of police protocol, then hit the recorder and announced the date and time.

Peter opened up proceedings. 'Sir Hugh, I would like to draw particular attention to a large payment out of your bank account.' Sir Hugh looked puzzled. Peter held up a data sheet and Sir Hugh's mobile phone. 'On the day of the court case, the twenty-second of May, you paid £300,000, supposedly, to Cynthia Bane-Everidge, your ex-wife.'

'What? It was supposed to be twenty grand not three hundred. Show me.'

Peter passed the data sheet over to Sir Hugh and his lawyer. They studied it carefully. Peter gave them a moment then carried on, 'There's another detail here. The account numbers don't tally up with your wife's account.'

Essence of Deceit by Mark Hall

Sir Hugh blurted out, 'This must be a mistake, surely? I just must have pressed an extra zero or something.'

'But the account number is different,' Peter pointed out.

'Oh, that is odd. It doesn't make sense. It's beyond me,' said Sir Hugh.

Peter pushed on. 'Did it not occur to you, Sir Hugh, that that was a lot of money paid out?'

'It is a lot of money, detective, and I know nothing about it!' Sir Hugh protested.

'Oh, come on, Sir Hugh—'

Sir Hugh interrupted the detective to put his point over. 'I do the finances once a month on the computer in the office. I do the staff wages, utility bills, pay my greedy wife and anything else needs dealing with. That's it, once a month, done.'

'Surely you must check your bank account now and again on the phone?' asked Peter. 'No, I don't. As I said, finances are done from the computer in the office. When I was last in the bank, one of the assistants put the app on my phone. I rarely use it, if ever.' He paused then asked for a small glass of water.

'No problem,' replied Peter. He nodded at Fergus to do the honours.

'Anyone else want one?' asked Fergus. Peter and the lawyer both said no. Fergus went to the water cooler to get one for himself and one for Sir Hugh.

'Everybody settled now?' Peter asked, and got straight back to it. 'Sir Hugh, is there anyone you know that has access to your computer, especially the banking?'

'No, nobody has access to the computer but me.'

'Are you absolutely sure? Can no one take over if you fall ill?'

Sir Hugh whispered to his lawyer, who indicated to his client to carry on. 'I did mention to Janice Brown that I would show her what to do and the general format, but, what with one thing and another, we never got around to it.'

Peter lifted up the data sheet. 'Also, on the same date that three hundred grand went out, fifty grand was paid to your butler, Reggie Milner, with a text: *Do not mention this to ANYONE and DO NOT mention it to ME EVER.*'

Sir Hugh looked aghast and stood up. 'This is utter rubbish. This is ridiculous.'

'We have a bit more that you need to listen to, Sir Hugh,' added Fergus.

Peter took a slightly different route in the questioning. 'How's your relationship with your wife, Cynthia?'

'It's okay. Cordial, I would say. She lives in Monaco in the south of France. I never see her. She has a new life and that's it.'

'What about your son? Gordon, isn't it?' asked Peter.

'He lives in Brighton with his girlfriend. We get on very well. I haven't seen him lately. He broke his leg playing rugby so he hasn't been able to visit but we keep in contact regularly. I'm sure you've got that in your data, detective.'

Peter nodded. 'We noticed that your son came and supported you on the day of the court case.'

'Yes, he did,' replied Sir Hugh. 'He's a good son, and his girlfriend is a good person as well, as a matter of fact. I'm sure he would've been here to support me now if he hadn't broken his leg soon after the court case.'

Essence of Deceit by Mark Hall

'Sir Hugh, said Peter, picking up the data sheet, 'the phone calls. You phoned Janice Brown moments before Reggie Milner was shot dead. You lured her away from the butler to give the assassin the golden opportunity to get rid of him. I feel that the fifty grand and the text to Reggie Milner was a bribe. My guess here, as the saying goes, was what the butler saw, and for you it was far too much. Fifty grand wasn't enough to shut him up so you had him shut up permanently.'

Sir Hugh was on his feet, screaming, 'This is madness! It's a goddam frame-up! Just because you didn't pin anything on me for the things that went on at the party, you now think that you can frame me for these murders.' Steven tried to regain some control.

'Give me a moment with my lawyer,' Sir Hugh growled.

Both detectives stood up and Peter turned his head. 'You got two minutes.' The pair stepped outside.

'He thinks he's a law unto himself,' Fergus pointed out.

'Too right there. I think we've got a fairly strong case,' Peter pondered.

The two detectives walked back into the room. Sir Hugh and his lawyer were surprisingly quiet.

Peter got stuck back in. He didn't want to lose momentum. 'Sir Hugh, when your dear friend, Clive Villiers, was shot, you'd invited him over for the evening. Villiers was sitting on the patio having lovely drinks in the warm evening sun. He was totally isolated. No one was around. You were on the phone, Sir Hugh, to your friend, Mr Vasquez, the Colombian. How very convenient. I'm also suggesting that you were in cahoots with Phil Atkins. A big payment out. Bring in a cleaner. Let's clean this place up. And, lo and behold. we have a hot shot on the staff.'

Sir Hugh shook his head. 'No way! Absolutely no way!'

'Also, a small detail that DC Ferguson and I noticed. You lectured Mary Edmunds on trust. You even got down the picture of Oliver Cromwell to make a point. Our point is that you had people removed that you couldn't trust. Binned. Eradicated. Cleaned up. Mary Edmunds left your office and Phil Atkins was lying in wait for her – for number five.'

'Total rubbish,' grunted Sir Hugh.

Peter concluded the interview, went through the protocol and instructed Sir Hugh Bane-Everidge that he would spend the next twenty-four hours in custody.

Essence of Deceit by Mark Hall

*

At the same time as the interview with Sir Hugh, Spyros and Claire questioned Diego Garcia in room one. Nothing had changed. Phone data was discussed and dissected and Diego's movements were brought under scrutiny. The CID pair gleaned nothing. They hadn't advanced any further. The chauffeur had stuck to the same story all the way through. The two detectives came to the unsatisfactory conclusion that there was no evidence of wrongdoing. But instinct told them otherwise. Something didn't seem right. Dave and Heather had also felt the same way when they'd spoken to Diego.

Clare and Spyros reluctantly ended the interview. Spyros gathered the paperwork, notes and data sheets, while Clare handed back the mobile phone to the chauffeur and announced, 'Mr Garcia, you're free to go.'

Happy, but slightly surprised, Diego asked, 'No more questions then?'

'Not at this moment in time,' replied Claire.

The trio left the interview room.

*

Essence of Deceit by Mark Hall

In interview room four, Dave and Heather had the company of Phil Atkins. Heather went through proceedings and hit the recording button. 'Interview with Mr Phil Atkins, employed by the Bane-Everidge Estate.'

Dave wasted no time. 'Mr Atkins, on the second of June, at the Bane-Everidge Estate, you were arrested in the possession of a firearm with intent to endanger life.'

'No comment,' Phil replied.

'Four murders, Mr Atkins. Was number five about to happen? Who was it this time? Jed Mullins? The gardener? Or was it Mary Edmunds? Sweet little Mary.'

Again, Phil replied, 'No comment.'

Dave was pacing around, working out his next question. 'Were you working for Sir Hugh and being paid a large sum of money to eradicate the people on the estate that Sir Hugh didn't trust, eh? Roland Van Mendes, the lawyer, Ben Charles, the chef, Reggie Milner, the butler, and Clive Villiers?'

Phil finally found his voice. 'You're not serious, are you? I haven't shot anyone. I'm totally innocent. I was mucking about. I wanted to scare Mary Edmunds. It was a prank.' Heather commented, 'Some prank with a loaded rifle.'

Phil continued, 'It wasn't loaded. I took the bullet out.'

'Forensics found a bullet in the rifle,' Heather stated.

Phil said that he'd thought he'd taken the bullet out then became confused and bewildered with all that was going on. 'I don't know what you're on about. Big payments from Sir Hugh? Why would he want his lawyer shot, who'd just defended him in a court case?'

'You tell us, Phil. Perhaps Sir Hugh couldn't trust him. You know that your boss had a thing about trust.' Dave stared down at Phil. 'Were you working with Sir Hugh or were you working on your own?'

Phil shook his head. 'Look, I haven't done any of this stuff. None of it. Someone jumped on my back. Yes, that's it. Someone jumped on my back and pushed into my neck. I couldn't breathe. I passed out. Next thing, this big cop, a man mountain with a massive gun, was arresting me, cuffing me and dragging me away in a cop car. I don't know a great deal about it because I was dazed.'

Dave responded, 'I really don't know what this world is coming to. You were lying in wait with a loaded rifle and you get apprehended by the police. It must've really spoilt your day.' He moved close up to Phil and held up mobile data his left hand. 'Listen, Phil, we have information here about you. We have a list of nasty threats from you. I'll read them to you. The first on your list is the chef, Ben Charles: *Watch your step or else.* The ex-chauffeur, Gary Hinchcliffe: *Be very careful, Gary.*'

Dave thumbed through the sheets. 'What else have we got? We have one to Jed Mullins: *You will be extremely sorry.* Oh, then you go all soppy, being very apologetic and talking about brotherly love. You have a nasty dig at Janice Brown too. Oh, there's another one: *You effing two-bit gardener. You don't know who you're messing with. Don't upset me, otherwise you'll end up with a bigger lump on your head than you have on your back, you ugly git.* Mr Atkins, you're a bit of a charmer. Come on, what's all this about?'

Phil wriggled in his chair. 'They're just threats to shut people up.'

Heather joined in, 'Shut people up, eh, Phil? Why do they need shutting up? What are you hiding?'

'I'm hiding nothing.'

Dave jumped in, 'Are you sure about that. You were seen at that fateful party after denying that you weren't there.'

Phil sighed loudly. 'Alright, I was in Scotland. I got back late so I nipped in to the party for about twenty minutes. I had one beer and a couple of nibbles and that's all. Then I went back to the sleeping quarters and to bed.'

Heather kept the pressure on. 'One, you failed to tell the police that you'd attended the party during previous questioning. Two, threatening texts. Three, arrested with a firearm.' Phil threw his arms up in surrender. 'I sold a bit of cocaine to Ben and Gary at the party.'

'You had a busy twenty minutes,' Heather added.

'Twenty minutes, half an hour, I don't know.'

'So you're a drug supplier then?' asked Dave.

'Hardly. I only supplied a bit.'

Dave took a mental note of 'possible supplier' but wanted to push Atkins on the three points. 'What happened next?'

'Ben got stroppy and aggressive ... started accusing me of ripping him off. He got right in my face. I wanted to give him a clump.' The anger that Phil was displaying was noted by both detectives.

Phil went on, 'That idiot Hinchcliffe made some comment. I cleared off. I didn't want to lose it. So, I went back to the sleeping quarters. I was still angry with the pair of bastards, especially Charlie boy, the chef, so I sent them a text each.'

Dave then asked, 'So why did Janice Brown get an aggressive text?'

Phil pushed his hands through his hair then tutted. 'She gets on my nerves, she does. Just because she runs the place, she wants to know everybody's business.'

'Carry on,' prompted Dave.

'Oh, she had to stick her five pennyworth in about the drugs. I got a lecture. I told her that it was only a little bit to Gary and Ben. She kept going on. We were outside the kitchen during a break so I walked off for a breather. I started chatting to the gardener, Archie. He was trimming a hedge a short distance from the kitchen. He had his usual Jack Daniels with him next to his other tools. Because I was a bit fed up, I thought I'd take a swig. I didn't even get it to my lips. He went off his head. He grabbed it off me and we had a tussle.

Carl saw us and broke it up. Later that day, I thought I'd send them both a text. If they got it in writing, they might take more notice.'

Dave started pacing the room again. 'Mr Atkins, it's our understanding that you supplied more drugs than your so-called 'little bit'. Also, that it doesn't take much for you to lose your temper and become aggressive. DC Barnes and I consider you to be a dangerous individual. You misled the police in earlier interviews, especially on your whereabouts regarding the party. Last, but by no means least, you were arrested with a firearm. The conclusion is this: there are two perpetrators in the midst of the Bane-Everidge Estate. You had no motive and it was very unlikely that you had an opportunity to shoot Roland Van Mendes, Reggie Milner and Clive Villiers. But you did have a motive to shoot Ben Charles.'

'No way!' shouted Phil.

Dave pushed on, 'No alibi, no witnesses. It was a perfect opportunity. Late at night, you rubbed him out. All done in the shadow of the other gunman. Plus Hinchcliffe disappeared into thin air. You also thought you had a chance to deal with Mary Edmunds, but that was poorly miscalculated.'

Phil shook his head and mumbled, 'No way.'

Essence of Deceit by Mark Hall

Dave nodded silently and decisively to Heather. Both detectives were now standing. Dave went through police procedure. 'Phil Atkins, you are arrested for possession of a loaded firearm with intent to endanger life. Also, for the murder of Ben Charles and the possession of a Class A drug with intent to supply. You do not have to say anything. But, it may harm your defence if you do not mention when questioned something which you later rely on in court. Anything you do say may be given in evidence. You will remain in custody until further notice.'

Two uniformed police officers entered the room and escorted Phil to a prison cell.

*

The CID team assembled back in the office. The detectives sat in their usual places. Peter stood at the incident board. 'Okay, team, I'll keep this fairly brief today.' He picked up a black felt pen and put a large tick next to Phil Atkins.

Spyros started clapping on his own. Peter acknowledged the fact and said, 'Thank you, Spyros. Phil Atkins, as you're all aware, is in custody. We've got a good case with the drug dealing, the threats, the shooting of Ben Charles and being caught red-handed with the firearm. So that's him out the way. What does concern me, which I'm not happy about, is that the uniform boys supposedly did a clean sweep of the whole goddamn estate but failed to find a rifle. I'll have a word with Sergeant Peters and Sergeant Hoskins. Perhaps, I'll go to the opticians and get a job lot of spectacles. Well, we still have the big fish to fry – Sir Hugh.'

Dave raised a few issues. 'There's still no sign of Gary Hinchcliffe and there's no clues about the assassin.'

'Have forensics traced any of those emails yet?' asked Clare.

Peter blew out loudly. 'There's still nothing on the emails and I don't like these loose ends not being tied up. Dave, take Claire and Spyros with you and have a poke round the sleeping quarters. The uniform boys should have done this thoroughly.' Peter tuts. 'If you want a job doing...'

*

At the Bane-Everidge Estate, Dave had briefed Janice about what they were doing and had received keys and a list of what room belonged to which staff member.

The three detectives painstakingly cracked on. They were in the room of Carl Watts. Spyros was moaning and Clare responded, 'I don't know what you're complaining about. Sergeant Hoskins and Sergeant Peters are gonna get roasted by DI Thompson. He's seething.'

Nothing out of the ordinary had appeared in the Carl's room, but Clare had searched diligently.

'You're just like a Jack Russell after a rabbit, Clare,' Spyros commented.

Claire responded with her usual manner, the glare, and then said, 'You'll do well, DC Papadakis, not to wind me up!' Spyros knew EXACTLY what she was referring to. The dip in the pool.

Dave didn't know what the pair were on about, but gave Spyros a sympathetic eyebrow raise in support.

The three detectives carried on from room to room. They searched the accommodation of Gina, Mary and Janice. Nothing raised suspicion, but pleasant comments were made when they looked at a picture of Janice with Robbie Williams at one of his concerts.

The detectives kept going through the rooms of Jed and Carl. No suspicions were raised. Jed had lots of football programmes and pictures of Fulham players which prompted Dave to say, 'Supporting a team like that is a crime. Perhaps we should nick him anyway.'

They arrived at the room of Diego and their anticipation went up. Dave opened the door. The trio searched with interest. They were convinced that they would find something but there was nothing to incriminate the chauffeur. There were some nice framed photographs of Diego with his family. Lots of photographs with his son. A photograph of Alfonso Vasquez and Diego with their two wives on a night out.

Clare held the photograph and studied it for a moment. 'Deffo close friends these two.'

Dave had a look too. 'Yeah, buddies alright.' They left the room.

'Last room,' announced Dave, 'and it belongs to Phil Atkins.'

The three CIDs were over the room like a rash. Within moments, Dave held up a five-foot-long plastic fishing rod case, which was empty. 'I'm sure that this would've housed the firearm. I'll take this to forensics, whether they want it or not.'

Drawers and cupboards were opened. Spyros pulled a face and reeled back. 'Jeeeezzzz!' He'd discovered a very mouldy cheese and onion roll in Phil's bedside drawer. 'Cor! It must've been there for months.'

Nothing else was found, other than the fishing bag. Satisfied, they left the room in order and shut the door. Spyros was holding a small supermarket bag with obviously something in it.

'Hello, what are you up to? What are you borrowing on a permanent basis?' asked Clare.

'It's the cheese and onion roll,' replied Spyros.

'What!' exclaimed Dave. 'Are you hungry or something?'

'No, no, it's not like that. I'm gonna find a bin for it. It's bad enough already but in another couple of days it'll stink the place out to high heaven.'

'We're off to see Archie Sangster, the gardener, now. Perhaps you can give it to him. He'll probably eat it,' Dave quipped. The detectives chuckled.

They walked past the kitchen and the bin area. Spyros launched the cheese roll towards a large wheelie bin where the lid was open leaving a gap of about six inches. It went straight in.

'Boom! Get in'! Claire did her usual jest of raising her eyebrows. At least it wasn't a glare, thought Spyros.

They carried on past the laundry building and the storage sheds and eventually came to the gardener's shed. Spyros tried the door. It was unlocked. Dave left the fishing bag outside and they all walked in.

'Tidy, very tidy,' Claire quipped.

'It's quite an upmarket shed – more of a log cabin,' remarked Dave. It was very compact with a kitchen area with a small sink and a small fridge, a tucked-away single bed up against the wall next to a chest of drawers.

Spyros looked at the books in a small bookcase. 'Napoleon Bonaparte, Winston Churchill, Abraham Lincoln. *A Gardener's Paradise*. What's this ... *Super Grass*?' a puzzled Spyros enquired. Dave and Claire turned their heads towards him. He burst out laughing. '*How to grow a fantastic lawn.*' Clare raised her eyebrows again.

Spyros was still poking about and dived in the chest of drawers by the bed. He found a crossword book, a book on British birds and a set of binoculars. He offered the binoculars to Dave who was leaning on the window sill, gazing out.

Dave took them. 'Well, these look a bit odd. The right lens looks a bit different to other one.' He looked through the binoculars. 'I can't focus these things. They're no good. Stick them back in the drawer.' Dave gently slung the binoculars at Spyros, who completely missed catching them and they fell down through the small gap between the bed and the wall.

Clare had a poke at Spyros. 'You couldn't catch a cold.'

Spyros groaned. 'How am I going to get them out? There's drawers underneath the bed.' He put in a lame effort to move the bed. 'Aw, gawd,' he moaned.

'Just leave it, Spyros,' Dave remarked. He returned to looking out the window. 'It's a good view from here. This is a lovely little spot – secluded – and that dozy gardener saw nothing.'

'Probably crashed out and drunk,' remarked Clare. She scanned the room. 'There's nothing here of interest.'

The door opened and in walked Archie. 'Oh, I've got uninvited guests. How nice. If I knew you were coming, I'd've baked a cake,' he said with a hint of sarcasm.

Dave wasted no time in starting a conversation with the gardener. 'Mr Sangster, this is a nice little hideaway, isn't it? A view of the whole estate, away from the rest of the staff.' Archie replied, 'Yeah, I love the peace. Shall I put the kettle on? Tea or coffee?'

Spyros was straight in. 'Coffee, please. No sugar.'

'Yeah, I'll have a coffee, please. No sugar,' replied Claire.

Dave tried to steer the gardener back to the conversation. 'Archie, listen. This is very important.'

Archie talked over Dave. 'Was it tea or coffee?'

'Tea will be great, thank you, Mr Sangster. You have a great view of the whole estate. Are you absolutely certain that you didn't see anything unusual or different or out of place? Anything that raised suspicion?'

Archie passed a mug of tea to Dave. 'Did you want sugar? I didn't put any in.'

Dave was beginning to get slightly irritated. Archie sat on a dining chair with his mug of tea. The three detectives waited for him to answer the question. Dave prompted, 'Well?' 'Oh, yeah. I told all you guys before, and your uniformed colleagues, that I didn't see anything at all. Nothing. You've got the killer though, haven't you?

Phil Atkins, who was caught with a firearm not far from the kitchen. And what about Sir Hugh? Is he still in custody?'

'Yeah, that's all ongoing, Mr Sangster,' replied Dave. He gulped his tea down and left the mug on the window sill. The other two detectives got the message that it was time to go. Spyros politely put his mug in the sink.

'You guys off already?' asked Archie.

'Yeah, gotta go. Duty calls,' commented Dave.

'Decent coffee that, Archie. I like that,' added Spyros.

Very good. Do you want to take some?' Archie offered.

'Nah, you're alright. Thanks for the offer,' declined Spyros.

The CIDs left the shed. Dave picked up the fishing bag. Archie followed with his mug of tea in his hand. 'Can I get you guys something from the greenhouse? We've got some wonderful tomatoes. They're really good.'

'No thanks,' replied Dave.

'What about some salad stuff? I'm sure you guys could take some of that. We've got cucumbers, nice lettuce, chillies. What about some chillies? Hey, what about some avocados?'

The CIDs were still slowly walking away. Claire appreciated Archie's kindness and felt slightly sorry for him as nobody was interested. Her male colleagues walked on as she turned and said to him, 'Archie, it's a very kind offer. But we're all okay. Thanks though.' She marched quickly to catch up with Spyros and Dave.

'Bit of a simpleton,' chipped in Spyros.

'He's just trying to be nice ... friendly,' added Claire.

'Yeah, guess so,' concluded Dave.

Archie sipped the remainder of his tea and watched the three detectives walk away.

*

Dave drove the four-by-four into the car park at HQ and the three detectives climbed out of the vehicle. They went into the building, and were very shortly in the office. It was all very busy. Dave noticed that Peter was in his private office. He headed there straight away, knocked on the door, and bowled in. 'I've got a present for forensics here.' He showed Peter the fishing rod bag. 'Phil Atkins kept his rifle in here. I'm sure Christine and her team would like to have a sniff around this.'

'Yeah, good stuff. It all helps the cause, I'm sure,' replied Peter.

Dave stood the bag up in the corner. Peter was studying his computer screen and Dave leaned over for a better look.

Peter explained what was going on. 'These are the images taken from the helicopter all around the grounds. They found zero. Uniformed boys scoured everywhere outside and found zero. They searched the house, the living quarters, the kitchen and rubbish bins, and they found zero. That's the explanation I've from Sergeant Hopkins and Sergeant Peters. They can't understand how they missed Phil Atkin's rifle. My only hope is that nothing else has been missed.'

Dave put his point of view over. ' Yeah, boss. They can find an ear stud but they can't find a firearm.'

Peter was still simmering. He growled, 'I've given them a severe talking-to. They need to sharpen up their acts. They're extremely lucky I didn't give the pair of them a written warning.' Peter looked at Dave. 'Steven Benson, Sir Hugh's lawyer, is on his way. He'll probably be here within an hour. Time for a team talk.'

In the main office, all the detectives took their usual seats. Dave, as usual, half sat on the desk next to Peter and the incident board.

'Guys, I do believe the finish line is in sight. Sir Hugh is our main man. I believe he'll also lead us to the assassin. For far too long, he's used his wealth and power to be above the law … untouchable. He may have got away with the party fiasco, but we'll nail him for three of the four murders. We'll get Phil Atkins, of course, for the other murder. Whether Sir Hugh was involved in the disappearance of Gary Hinchcliffe, or whether he did retire out of sight, miles from anyone, we'll still investigate.'

Peter stood up. 'Fergus, Claire and Spyros, carry on looking for Gary Hinchcliffe. Dave and Heather, come with me to interview room one. Steven Benson will be here shortly, and we can go and see our friend, Sir Hugh.'

The detectives got settled and organised and ready in the interview room. There were three chairs for the detectives. On the other side of the desk, there were two chairs. Dave and Heather sat down and Peter started pacing.

Essence of Deceit by Mark Hall

Heather whispered to Dave, 'The lull before the storm. I wish the boss would sit down. All this pacing around is making me dizzy. Come to think of it, you're a bit of a pacer. Perhaps you two could do a sponsored pace challenge for charity.'

Dave whispered a sarcastic, 'Ha, ha!'

There was a knock at the door. Sir Hugh walked in accompanied by a police officer. He sat down at the desk. Moments later, Steven Benson came in. Peter stood between Heather and Dave and in front of Sir Hugh and his lawyer. Police protocol and recorded procedures were dealt with.

'Sir Hugh, I'd like to clarify a couple of points. We don't believe that you had any connection with Phil Atkins and the death of Ben Charles. That's a totally separate case. But I am arresting you on suspicion of the murders of Roland Van Mendes, Reggie Milner and Clive Villiers. You paid out £300,000 to an unknown person to complete the task. You
also assisted the killer by isolating two of the victims through mobile phone calls, thereby creating a window of opportunity. You tried to silence Reggie Milner with a £50,000 bribe. When you feared that wouldn't work, you had him silenced permanently.'

Peter continued, 'You do not have to say anything. But, it may harm your defence if you do not mention when questioned something which you later rely on in court. Anything you do say may be given in evidence.'

Steven stood up. 'My client is innocent of all charges. And none of these charges will stick.'

'Your client will remain in custody until the court hearing. Bail is refused,' Peter instructed.

'This is all wrong,' barked Sir Hugh. 'You're all a bunch of fools. I need to get back to the estate.' Steven raised a hand in a gesture to tell Sir Hugh to remain silent. He considered that was the best course of action, Any more protesting would be very damaging.

'I'm sure that Janice Brown will be more than capable of running the day-to-day affairs of the Bane-Everidge Estate,' Peter mentioned to Sir Hugh.

The three detectives stood up. On cue, two police officers entered the room. Sir Hugh was escorted out, followed by Steven. Heather picked up the equipment used in the interview and followed Peter and Dave out of the room.

In the main office, the team of six were all there and the mood was upbeat. Peter made his way to the front of the office, full of good emotions. He took a moment. 'Well, team—'

Clare stood up. 'Let's hear it for the boss!'

The whole team stood up and noisily applauded. Peter took it upon himself to go around and shake everybody's hand and give them a hug.

POP! Spyros opened a champagne bottle. Clare also opened a bottle, the flying cork missing Fergus's head by a couple of inches. He reacted with a bit of Glaswegian language, which produced a few laughs. Heather dished out plastic cups from the water cooler. Spyros and Claire poured out the fizz.

Peter got back to the front of the office and held his cup ready for a toast. 'I would just like to say that it's been a long difficult journey. But with your hard work and dedication we've got rid of two very unsavoury individuals. They both treated the law with contempt. One was an opportunist rat lurking in the shadows, the other hid behind wealth and power. So I, therefore, raise my glass, sorry, plastic cup…' A couple of laughs were heard. 'to the team of six.'

'THE TEAM OF SIX!' everybody toasted.

A little later, the office was buzzing. Peter chatted with Spyros and Heather.

Heather raised an issue. 'So, Janice Brown will be running the show down there. Is she going to be lady of the manor, I wonder?'

'Sir Hugh has an ex-wife who lives in the south of France and a son who lives in Brighton. I'm sure they'll sort it out. I'm going to leave it for a day two then pop down there to have a chat with Janice and see how things are going,' replied Peter. He got up and had a general mingle with the other team members. After about thirty minutes, he clapped his hands. 'Okay, it's about five o'clock. Let's wrap it up today. See you in the morning. Have a good evening.'

The team didn't have to be told twice. They were all off out the office. Even Dave didn't hang about. The office became quiet and still. Peter looked around the office. He looked at the incident board, then he walked to his private office and tapped on the email inbox. His wife's voice entered his head. 'You never switch off, do you? Always the detective.' Right, that was it. He should get off home, he thought. But there was an email. That pulled him in and screamed JOB DONE! He paused then pressed the speed dial for forensics on his desk phone.

Immediately, the call was answered. 'Hello, Eugene speaking.'

'Hi, Eugene. DI Thompson here. I've had an anonymous email. Did you trace any of those emails?'

'Not as yet. Whoever is hiding behind them is very smart. This is such a difficult one.'

'Do you want me to open this?' asked Peter.

'Yeah, go ahead and read it out.'

The job is done it's been completed

Now the guilty have been deleted

I have done the task you didn't do

I was very thorough and seen it through

Justice and truth are finally here

Replacing corruption, lies and fear.

'Wow!' exclaimed Eugene. 'That's obviously the killer from the Bane-Everidge Estate.'

'Yeah, no prizes for guessing that one. Whoever it is seems to revel in the whole scenario,' Peter declared.

Christine came on the line. 'Like Eugene said, we just can't find any trace of these emails, but obviously we'll keep looking. Sorry we couldn't help further.'

Disappointed, Peter thanked both of them and clicked off the phone. He then turned the computer off.

*

A couple of days later, some of the team were on the Hinchcliffe case. Peter and Heather discussed the email. 'We could discuss this till we're blue in the face and still not get any further. Forensics have not gained an inch on these emails. It's so frustrating.' Peter stood up. 'Right, Heather. Let's grab Fergus. We're going for a little drive … I'm sure you know where to.' He gave Dave a very quick update, then strode out of the office and left the building with Fergus and Heather.

It was a quiet drive to the Bane-Everidge Estate. It was certainly unusual for Fergus not to be rabbiting on, thought Peter. The four-by-four pulled up close to the steps leading to the house.

The three detectives got to the front door and Peter rang the bell. Gina opened the door.

'How's things?' enquired Peter.

'Okay, I suppose. Sir Hugh's son, Gordon, has moved in with his girlfriend, Phoebe. I don't know how long for.'

'It could be a very long time, Gina,' replied Peter.

'Oh!' Gina paused to digest the news. She displayed a lack of emotion that the three detectives noticed. 'If you follow me, we can go to the office. Gordon is in there,' Gina suggested.

'Okay, lead on,' Peter replied.

Gina knocked on the door of the office and there was a muffled 'Come in'. She walked off and left the detectives to it. They entered the office. Gordon Bane-Everidge struggled to stand up out of his chair due to his broken leg, which was plastered up. Peter introduced himself and his colleagues.

'The leg's on the mend, thankfully. It's a bit of an effort getting in and out of chairs,' said Gordon. 'My girlfriend, Phoebe, and I drove up here a couple of days ago to keep an eye on things. I thought it might be short term, but I'm coming to the conclusion it may be permanent.'

Peter responded with, 'Very likely, Gordon, it will be permanent. So, this is all yours then?'

'Yes, it is. When my parents divorced, which was about twelve years ago, I was … let me think … er… twenty-three years old. I'm now thirty-five. My father had an agreement drawn up, passing the estate onto me. My mother was in absolute total agreement. Her words were, "Good that suits me. I don't like the weather here. I don't like the people here. I'm off to start a new life in the south of France where the weather is warm and the people are sunny, not like here. I'll be glad to see the back of England."'

Heather listened intently then asked, 'Are you still in contact with your mother, Gordon?'

'Yes, not massive amounts, but we keep in touch. I've been to France a few times.' Fergus joined in, 'Did you mention to your mother about the goings-on here?'

'I did but she's totally not interested. I believe she's still speaking to my father, albeit very occasionally.'

'It's quite a task, taking this place on, Gordon,' Peter suggested.

'Yeah, it's a bit intimidating. The recent episodes have affected the staff, as you can imagine. I won't be doing as much entertaining as my father. There won't be so many dignitaries visiting and there certainly won't be so many parties. It's unlikely that I'll get a butler. And I'm not too sure whether I'll keep the chauffeur. Janice Brown might leave, but she's not decided. Mary Edmunds is leaving in two days' time and the gardener, Archie Sangster, is leaving tonight. I might need one or two general staff though. And of course a gardener cum handyman. So, it's very much up in the air.'

'Good luck with all that,' remarked Peter. He then indicated to Fergus and Heather that it was time to move.

'Okay, Gordon. Thanks for the update. My team and I just want to have a final walk round the estate and have a quick chat with one or two of the staff. Is that okay?'

'Be my guest,' replied Gordon. 'You know where I am.'

The three detectives left the office and walked through the house. They bumped into Janice. She proceeded to tell the detectives about her plans for the future, adding that she was undecided. Peter then asked about the new gaffer.

'He's fine. He's very nice, actually, and his girlfriend, Phoebe, is very pleasant. I started work here ten years ago. A few months later, Gordon moved out to live in Brighton and go to the university down there but he's been back and forth few times.'

Peter jumped straight in. 'What? Back for the parties?'

'Oh no, definitely not. He's not a party person. He's quite quiet and reserved. He used to come here with Phoebe to see his father. If the weather was half decent, Gordon and Phoebe would spend a lot of time in the pool.'

Mary emerged from the nearby study. The three detectives listened to Mary's plans and tried to glean information about the new couple becoming the heads of Bane-Everidge Estate.

*

Archie was busy preparing to leave the Bane-Everidge Estate. A suitcase was open on the bed. There wasn't a great deal to pack and it didn't take him long.

The suitcase shut and standing by the door, Archie went to the fridge and took out a few remnants. Half a carton of milk. He made sure the lid was on tight and put it into a carrier bag then he added an open jar of marmalade and a pack of Flora and an unopened packet of cheddar cheese. He put the carrier bag next to his suitcase at the door, cleaned out the fridge and turned it off.

Archie had a good look round. He went through the cupboards and drawers and decided to leave the tea and coffee. The sink was clean. The bedclothes were stuffed into a large blue plastic laundry bag. Job done. Time to go. He headed towards the kitchen and laundry area. He wasn't one for great goodbyes and liked to keep things minimal. The kitchen was his first stop. The suitcase and laundry bag were left at the door.

Archie waddled into the kitchen with the carrier bag. He greeted Jed and Carl with, 'Good morning. I've a few bits here.'

'Put them in the fridge, Archie.' The kitchen boys stopped what they were doing and went over to Archie.

'I hear you're off then?' said Jed.

'Yeah, I've had enough really. I'm no spring chicken anymore and all the stuff going on here has been very upsetting. I'm off to Ontario. I think I'm gonna do a lot of fishing and maybe get a little part-time job.'

'Gardening?' asked Carl.

'Maybe. Small scale, though. Nothing like this place. Oh well, boys, it's been nice knowing you.' Archie shook their hands. 'All the best, boys.'

'You take care, Archie. Safe journey. Hope it all works out well for you. mate,' Jed and Carl replied.

Archie went out of the kitchen, grabbed the suitcase and the laundry bag and went into the laundrette. The four machines were in action. He plonked the bag on a small table.

Gina came in, wheeling a laundry trolley. 'Archie, Archie.' She put her arms round the gardener or soon-to-be-ex-gardener. 'You're off then? You're leaving now?'

'Yeah, on my way. Canada's calling…'

'Moose and mountains then. No more stuck-up upper classes to be around. It sounds great, Archie. I'd love to come with you. Mary's leaving in the next day or so and Janice might go too, but I reckon she'll change her mind.'

Archie wanted to get away. 'Gina, it's been a pleasure.' He leaned forwards and gave Gina a light kiss on the cheek. 'Bye, Gina, take care. Look after yourself, yeah?'

'Bye, Archie.'

Essence of Deceit by Mark Hall

The soon-to-be-ex-gardener, suitcase in hand, waddled through the house heading towards the office to say goodbye to Gordon. He wanted to say goodbye to Janice and Mary but time was getting on and he had a plane to catch.

*

Peter, Heather and Fergus were walking around the swimming pool area. The detectives had had a good walk around inside the house, now they were doing a tour of the outside. They planned to end up having a quick chat with the kitchen staff and Archie Sangster.

*

Archie knocked on the door of the office and opened it slightly.

'Hello, come in.' Gordon was already standing. 'You're off now then? You're leaving a lot earlier than I thought. I didn't think you were leaving until late tonight,' he exclaimed. 'I got an earlier flight booked,' replied Archie.

'You know that there's three CID here, having another nose around?'

'Yeah, I saw that. Everything is tight,' replied Archie. 'Well, it took a couple of years to settle in here. It was some time ago that we met in Jamaica and I gave you my contact number and you managed to persuade your father to take me on.'

'Well, there was a vacancy and you had all the right credentials,' answered Gordon with a wry smile. 'Including you going over to the dark side.'

'Well, I wouldn't call it that. More like the good side. Getting rid of the bad stuff. Clearing out the trash,' Archie pointed out.

Gordon agreed, 'Yes, you're dead right, Archie. I was in my teenage years and at one of Dad's parties when I was abused by Clive Villiers and Roland Van Mendes. I told my father, who did absolutely nothing, just told me to keep quiet. He didn't want the place tarnished. He was a big government official. I felt ill for months. I felt betrayed by my father. I was disgusted. Villiers and Van Mendes were absolutely revolting. I'm sure that there were others who'd had the same experience as me, but of course it was all covered up. I knew I would get my revenge. I bided my time. I was the perfect, lovable, wonderful son.'

Archie listened intently as Gordon unravelled the sinister goings-on at the Bane-Everidge Estate.

'I never went to another party – and there were plenty. At the last party, Ben Charles, the chef, totally off his head on cocaine, threw that guy off the balcony to his death. He also tried to do the same with one of the three girls who went missing. Two of the girls managed to fight Ben off. My so-called father and Van Mendes saw the whole episode and just called it "party entertainment". It's just unbelievable. The three girls vanished into thin air … they just fell off the map. Of course, my father and Van Mendes had something to do with it but they were untouchable. How do I know all this?'

'Go on,' prompted Archie, looking at his watch.

'Because Gary Hinchcliffe turned up on my doorstep, extremely distressed, and told me everything. We'd got on very well when I was at the estate. I told him that I'd deal with Ben Charles. Hinchcliffe said that he was going live in Cornwall and was going to disappear off the radar. I'd never hear or see him again. Sadly, I respected his wishes. I then decided that enough was enough and the time was right.'

*

Essence of Deceit by Mark Hall

The three detectives spoke to Jed and Carl in the kitchen. They didn't learn anything they didn't already know. They left the kitchen and made their way towards the gardener's shed. Peter knocked on the door. There was no answer so he tried the handle. It was unlocked so they all walked in. Peter remarked that it was a shame that the gardener wasn't there. Without further ado, Fergus was into everything. Not that there was a great deal in there as the cupboard doors and drawers were already open.

*

Time was moving on and Archie was mindful that his taxi to the airport would soon be there. 'How come I had to remove Reggie Milner?' he asked.

Gordon took a breath then answered, 'I set all that up by coming into this office and using my father's computer. I knew his password to get into his bank account so I paid your £300,000 fee. But I got caught by Reggie Milner. Thank God he didn't know what I was doing exactly, but he saw my father's bank account on the screen and that was enough for him to start bribing me. I had to chuck him fifty grand to keep him quiet. Then it got very tricky. I managed to get hold of the old man's mobile and sent Reggie a text to shut him up. He nearly blew the lid off the whole thing. By using my father's mobile, I thought I was covering my tracks, but somehow Reggie got hold of my mobile number and started demanding more money. There was no other option. He had to go.'

*

In the gardener's shed, Fergus had a little find. A half-full bottle of Jack Daniels. 'Oh, don't mind if I do, Mr Sangster,' he said. Peter was ready to go. Fergus opened the whisky and dropped the cork between the bed and the wall. He cursed. 'Hold this, please, Heather.' She obliged.

Peter was beginning to get restless. 'Do come on, Fergus. I'd like to see Archie Sangster before he goes.'

'That won't be until later, according to Gordon,' Fergus replied, pulling out the drawers from under the bed and eventually squeezing the bed out.

Heather started to wonder about Archie. 'Well, he did say his final goodbyes to the kitchen boys.'

Fergus got the cork. 'Hey, what's this?' he exclaimed. He stood up, holding the cork and a pair of binoculars. Heather put the cork in the bottle. Fergus looked at the binoculars. 'These are a bit odd. It looks like he's done a makeshift repair. The right lens looks fairly decent.' He walked towards the window and looked out. At the same time, a people carrier taxi turned up for Archie.

'Fergus, try focusing on that taxi that's just pulled up,' said Heather.

'These are rubbish! They aren't any good,' declared the Scotsman.

Peter was surprised that the taxi had turned up so soon. 'Great,' he said sarcastically. 'I wouldn't have minded a little chat with Archie Sangster before he left. We don't have anything on him,' he pondered.

*

Archie looked at his watch and calculated that the taxi must have arrived, Gordon took it as a cue that the 'gardener' was about to leave. The pair walked slowly to the door.

'I'm glad you got rid of Phil Atkins. He wasn't on the list though. Do you want paying for that?' Gordon mentioned.

'Have it as a freebie. He was a complete wrong one. He was nothing but trouble. I'm sure that if I hadn't dealt with him, you'd have called me back in the future.' They walked through the office door into the reception area. 'It's a shame that I never said goodbye to Mary and Janice,' mused Archie.

'Don't worry. I'll tell them. Don't you want to say goodbye to the police?'

'I already have. I've been keeping them up to date with emails.' Archie winked at Gordon.

*

The trio of CIDs stood at the window in the gardener's shed. Peter held his hand out. 'Pass those binoculars over, Fergus.'

'I told you, they're no good,' replied Fergus.

Peter looked closely at the binoculars. 'Well, what has he done here? This is interesting.'

Heather passed the Jack Daniels to the Glaswegian as she became more interested in her boss and the binoculars. 'It looks like a different lens on the right than on the other side,' she pointed out.

Peter put the binoculars to his eyes and looked through them. He kept fiddling with them. 'Hold on a minute, hold on. Wow, if you shut your left eye, this right lens is very powerful. Heather, take a note of Cummings Airport Taxis. I'll read out the registration.' He couldn't believe how powerful this lens was. 'Take a look, Heather. The detail you can get from this is incredible.'

*

Gordon and Archie were at the front door. 'Goodbye, Gordon.' The pair shook hands.

'Goodbye, Brad. Where are you going?' asked Gordon.

'A place for a Newman,' replied Brad Newman. 'No more Archie Sangster. No more gardener. I can't tell you where I'm going because I might have to kill you. It's not Ontario. Adios, Gordon.'

'Ciao, Brad.'

Brad Newman strutted down the steps of the house to the waiting taxi.

*

Heather was also amazed how powerful the lens was. She handed the binoculars back to her boss. Peter fixed his eye on the taxi. The instinct of the detective slowly started to stir. The taxi driver slid back the large side door and opened up the boot. He watched intently then mumbled, 'Something just doesn't smell right.'

Essence of Deceit by Mark Hall

The ex-gardener strutted down the steps of the house, put his case in the back and shut the door. The driver climbed in the front as his passenger climbed in through the side door and pulled it shut.

'Looks like he's away then,' exclaimed Fergus. 'Here's to you, Mr Gardener.' He took the top off the Jack Daniels and took a big swig. 'Paaaaaaaaa! Jeeeeezzz! This ain't Jack Daniels.' He took another small sip just to confirm. 'It's goddamn cold tea! What the hell is he carrying that around for? A bottle of cold tea? It doesn't make any sense.'

Peter was half-listening to Fergus but his attention was aroused by how Archie had walked down the steps with great ease. The boss turned to his two colleagues. 'Something isn't right. I've just seen the waddling Archie Sangster bounce down those steps like a young gazelle.'

'Yeah and what's this lark with the tea in a Jack Daniels bottle?' Fergus added. Peter's attention was now drawn to the binoculars. There were two discrete clips keeping the two lens attached. He unfastened the clips, took a tissue from his pocket and cleaned the lens barrel. 'Oh my God! Oh ... my ... God!' he exclaimed. The penny was beginning to drop. He raised his voice.

'This is a very high-powered elite rifle telescope, extremely hard to come by. It's been disguised as busted binoculars, but it's ready to unhook as required. Very clever.'

Heather looked astonished as did Fergus. 'Archie Sangster has been a total act, a deception. He's been portraying the image of a heavy drinking simpleton, hampered by physical problems. It's the total opposite,' she said, nailing the conclusion. The three detectives were silent. There was nothing more to add.

They weren't silent for long. Peter snapped back into action, barking orders. 'Heather, ring Cummings Airport Taxis. Have you got Archie Sangster's mobile?'

'Yes,' she replied.

'Well done, good. Find him as well. Let's have a word with Gordon.'

The three detectives climbed up the steps. Heather was a couple of paces behind, on the mobile phone. Peter rang the bell for a long time. Gordon answered the door holding a freshly lit cigar.

Peter and Fergus barged their way in, while Heather stayed outside. 'What do you know about Archie Sangster, the bloody gardener?'

Gordon puffed out a large amount of smoke, trying to keep it away from the detectives. 'Nothing. There was nothing to know about him. He was a loner, always busy around the grounds. My father hired him. He kept himself to himself. Why? Is there some sort of problem, detective?'

Peter was at boiling point. Through gritted teeth, he said to Gordon, 'We have a very strong suspicion, almost a certainty, that Archie Sangster is the assassin.'

Gordon's acting skills were sublime. 'You've got to be joking! Are you sure, gentlemen? Really, this is unbelievable! I can't see that, not in a million years. As I say, I know nothing about him. My father hired him.'

Peter was getting more impatient. He asked, 'Where's he heading to now then? Do you know that?'

'He's flying to Ontario from Heathrow Airport,' Gordon replied.

'I don't suppose you know flight number or time of departure?' Fergus asked.

'No, sorry, gents. That's all I know.'

'Come on, Fergus. Let's go.' Peter and Fergus started to move rapidly down the steps. Peter turned to look at Gordon and shouted, 'We'll be in touch.'

The three detectives ran to the four-by-four. 'What's happening?' gasped Heather.

'Heathrow Airport!' Fergus blurted out.

*

Gordon stood on the top step of the house. He watched the frantic detectives leave, the vehicle speeding off. As the new king of the estate, his eyes slowly scanned the kingdom he'd acquired. He drew deeply on his cigar, blew out a large plume of smoke, and, with a great feeling of satisfaction, went in and shut the door.

*

In the detective's vehicle, it was frantic. Heather had had no contact with Cummings Airport Taxis or Archie Sangster. 'Sir, these numbers just don't exist.'

'Great,' replied Peter. He then instructed Heather to phone Heathrow Airport, then phone all the other airports and alert airport security, passenger lists, CCTV, anything they could think of.

Essence of Deceit by Mark Hall

Fergus was already busy alerting police forces within the surrounding areas and beyond. In a very brief break from the phone calls, he remarked, 'We've got the big man, Sir Hugh. Surely that's the main thing? And that weasel, Phil Atkins.'

'Yeah, but if we get Archie Sangster, that'll certainly tie all the loose ends up,' Peter responded. Fergus went back on the phone.

The traffic started to slow down. There was a large tailback. That was all they needed, Peter thought. He took some comfort in the fact that they had the big man, then felt a very sharp dig from an irritating email that came to mind, which referred to the infamous party. And, even more frustratingly, seemed to fit recent events.

...compelling evidence was staring you in the face. If you had looked hard enough instead of being blind...

*

In Cummings Airport Taxis, the atmosphere was jovial. The driver, Cyril Clark, knew his passenger, Brad Newman, quite well. They'd been friends for many years. Cyril had occasionally done a job for Brad. He spent most of his time living in Jamaica with his wife Sandra. 'Hey, Brad, I'm going to pull off to go down this country lane. It's a quiet wooded area. I have to do a few alterations, if you know what I'm saying ...'

'I've got to do the same, Cyril. Gotta brush up. I've got to look buff for your missus, Cyril. I can't be eating Sandra's wonderful jerk chicken with the hump.'

Cyril roared with laughter, slapped his thigh and said, 'You kill me, man!' He turned down the small country lane, pulled off the road and stopped the engine.

The two of them got to work. Cyril carefully peeled off the plastic Cummings Airport Taxis sticker, which was all round the vehicle, and Brad removed his brown and grey hairpiece and small thin goatee beard. Cyril pulled off the false plastic registration plates. He then put everything into a clear bin bag. Brad unhinged his plastic hump on his back. He then proceeded to put it in the plastic bag together with his hairpiece and his small beard.

Cyril laughed. 'Hey, man. You look like a hot geezer. You look twenty years younger. I might not allow you to drink beer at my place.' He laughed again, then went quickly to the back of the people carrier and lifted up the carpet to reveal a small compartment. He brought out a small bottle of acid, grabbed the plastic bag and walked about thirty feet into the woods. Very carefully, he emptied the acid on the bag and dropped the empty bottle on the top. The chemical reacted straight away. Hissing and spitting and sending up steam.

In a few minutes, there was nothing left. Cyril was satisfied, moved swiftly back to the vehicle and climbed in.

' Let's go, bro!' exclaimed Brad.

*

The atmosphere in the detectives' four-by-four was a potent mixture of frustration and bewilderment. Peter was struggling to keep his anger below the surface. Heather and Fergus were doing their upmost on their mobile phones to trace the taxi and Archie Sangster.

Heather was speaking to Heathrow Airport security and Peter butted straight in, 'Well, tell security to check EVERY people carrier that comes into the goddamn parking and drop-off area.'

The CIDs were trying every avenue and option but kept running into a dead end.

Fergus spoke up, 'Sir, all the police forces and all the airport securities are on high alert. Also, at the other end, security at Ontario

International Airport have been given the heads up. I'm sure we've covered all bases.'

But Peter knew that the so-called Mr Sangster was far too slick and smart to leave an obvious trail. The traffic started to slow down again. The look of resignation on the detectives' faces said it all.

*

Cyril Clark put his foot down on the open motorway. 'Gatwick, here we come. Then on to sunny Jamaica. Yeeehaaaa! You gonna stay with us for a while, Brad? Or have you got another job?'

'Well, if that's alright, Cyril, I'll stay with you for a few days then I'll move further north up the island. I've got a friend I'm gonna see.'

'Business or pleasure?' asked Cyril.

'Deffo pleasure. Hard-working boy like me and all the stress I've had,' replied Brad.   Cyril started to laugh. 'And what's her name then?'

'Sabrina. Just good ole Sabrina.'

Cyril started to laugh a bit more. 'Hey, bro, you're something else. I reckon all the women are on red alert when you come over.'

Essence of Deceit by Mark Hall

He then slapped the steering wheel and laughed louder. Then his voice took on a more serious note. 'Brad, when we get to the drop-off point, my mate Dukie will take care of this bus, so obviously we need to be slick and quick. The place'll be crawling with police. Passports and tickets are all sorted. I'll give them to you very shortly.'

'Thanks, Cyril, you wizard. I love ya,' replied Brad.

'Brad, I've got something for you.' Cyril briefly fiddled with the audio system on the dashboard. 'I know this is one of your favourites, it's called Down Time by Errol Finbar' Cyril turned the volume up and joined in.

Work is finished the tools are down

I'm dressed up heading for town

find me a bar with a touch of class

friendly bar staff to fill my glass

want a good time, have some fun

Might stay late and greet the rising sun .

END

Essence of Deceit by Mark Hall